THE
GIRLS *of*
VICTORY STREET

THE
GIRLS *of*
VICTORY STREET

PAM HOWES

bookouture

Published by Bookouture in 2020

An imprint of Storyfire Ltd.
Carmelite House
50 Victoria Embankment
London EC4Y 0DZ

www.bookouture.com

ISBN: 978-1-83888-000-2
eBook ISBN: 978-1-78681-977-2

Dedicated to the memory of Bobby Vee (April 1943–October 2016), who I always had in mind when I created the character of Bobby Harrison in this story.
Thank you for the wonderful music and the fabulous memories of meeting you. A time I will always treasure.

Chapter One

Wavertree, February 1939

Bella Rogers groaned as the alarm clock rang out on the bedside table. Monday morning – again. It came around all too quickly. She rolled onto her side, turned off the clanging bell and pulled her share of the thin woollen blankets around her. The air in the room felt icy cold and she shivered. Her nose, the only bit of her outside the blankets, was freezing.

She drew her legs up as her younger sister Molly's cold feet touched her shins. The three Rogers sisters all topped and tailed in the big double bed, and now little Betty snuggled down into Bella's back. Bella screwed her eyes shut again and tried to recapture the dream she'd been enjoying. *Just five more minutes*, she begged silently as she listened to her mam and dad moving around in their bedroom across the landing, and then the sound of them hurrying downstairs to start their day.

Soon her mam would be yelling up the stairs for the sisters to hurry up and get dressed. It was no use; the dream had gone, and there was no more losing herself in thoughts of Bobby Harrison chasing her across The Mystery Park on a warm summer's day, catching hold of her and pulling her into his arms. Not that she'd yet had that pleasure, but with his big blue eyes and floppy blond hair, he was the most handsome boy in the school and every girl's dream of a sweetheart. He was also the most popular singer in the church choir and people said he sang like an angel. Bella loved to sing alongside him; everybody said they harmonised well.

She sighed and stared up at the cracks in the ceiling, just visible in the early morning light filtering through the thin curtains. She might as well as get up and make a start. She could hear her dad clearing the grate and riddling the ashes. Soon he'd have a roaring fire going that would take the chill off the back sitting room. She stuck a foot out of bed and winced as she waved it around, testing the air. Molly sat up slowly, pushing her dark brown fringe out of her sleepy eyes.

'Morning, Mol,' Bella greeted her sister, who scratched her nose and sniffed loudly. 'It's freezing,' she complained. She handed a handkerchief to Molly and climbed out of bed, gingerly stepping onto the cold, worn lino, and crossed to the window. Drawing back the curtains, she gasped as she gazed out onto the backyard, which was covered in a thick snowfall. She chipped at the feathers of ice that had formed patterns on the glass with her fingernail. 'It's been snowing hard again. Best throw your clothes on right away,' she said to Molly. 'Here, do it under the blankets and keep warm.' She passed one of the three neatly folded piles of clothes that her mam had left out last night across to Molly and shook Betty gently by the shoulder. 'Come on, Bets. Let's get you dressed and then we'll go down and have some breakfast.'

Betty's large brown eyes flew open and her bottom lip pouted. 'I want to stop in bed today,' she said. 'Don't wanna go to school.'

Bella smiled. 'You have to. We'll soon have you warmed up. Come on, Daddy's making a nice fire before he goes to work and Mam will be making porridge to warm you up before we go out.'

She sat down on the bed, lifted Betty on to her knee and pulled off her flannel nightdress. Betty's skinny arms, covered in goose-bumps, huddled around her little body and her teeth chattered as Bella slipped a fleecy liberty bodice over a vest and knickers, followed by a white blouse, navy gymslip and a warm dark blue cardigan knitted by their mam. Bella did her best to help as much as she could with her younger sisters as both their parents worked hard and had little spare time. Their dad would be heading off to his job as a tram driver shortly and Mam worked at Olive Mount children's hospital, just up the road, as a cleaner. She too would be leaving the house soon as she began her shift at eight o'clock. She finished at three, which gave her just enough time to get home and tidy up before she picked up five-year-old Betty from infant school at half past three.

Bella, who would be fifteen next month, and twelve-year-old Molly walked home together as they didn't finish until four.

Bella told Molly to help Betty put her socks on and take her downstairs to Mam while she got dressed herself. She hurriedly threw on her white blouse, grey pleated skirt and cardigan, and took a look in the age-speckled mirror on the wardrobe door. She'd do. There wasn't much choice. Her school clothes were all she had to wear during the week. Mam had knitted them all thick woollen socks as part of their Christmas presents and although they were hardly the height of fashion, they were warm and would keep the chilblains at bay on a day like today when her feet were shoved inside her wellies. She didn't have any other boots that would do in this weather.

Bella quickly made the bed; she picked up their discarded nighties from the floor and folded them before slipping them under the pillows. She pulled a brush through her dark, wavy hair, smoothing down her glossy fringe, and teased out the ends so that they sat on her shoulders in curled flicks. She clipped the sides back behind her ears with a couple of tortoiseshell hair slides and, satisfied that it looked okay, ran down the stairs to join her sisters.

The ice was beginning to melt on the windows as the warmth from the roaring fire worked its way around the small back sitting room. Betty and Molly were seated at the table eating breakfast and their mam was rushing around as usual, handing a greaseproof wrapped package of sarnies to Dad with a flask of tea for his dinner break.

'Right, you sit down, our Bella,' Mam ordered. 'I'll get you a bowl of porridge.'

Bella smiled. Although her mam had insisted she be christened Annabelle, she was always called 'our Bella' at home and her friends called her Bella too.

'You off now, Dad?' Bella threw her arms around him and gave him a hug. 'Don't work too hard.'

'I'll do me best not to, queen,' he teased. His deep-set brown eyes, the same colour as all his daughters', twinkled and he gave her a hug back. 'See youse all later, gels,' he said, pecking Mam on the cheek and tweaking Molly and Betty's plaits, which had miraculously survived a night in bed without needing redoing. He hurried down the narrow hallway to the front door with their shouted goodbyes following him.

Bella sat down next to Molly, sprinkled sugar over her porridge and wolfed it down in seconds flat. She eyed up the last slice of toast left on a plate in the middle of the table and hoped no one else wanted it. Good manners made her ask her sisters if they wanted to share but they shook their heads. She reached for the toast and spread a thin layer of mixed fruit jam across the surface.

The label on the jam, bought from the corner shop on Victory Street, gave no clue as to what the fruit might be, but Bella thought she detected apple and possibly plum. Mrs Horner, who ran the shop, made a lot of jams and chutneys and gave a halfpenny back for every empty jar that was returned to her. The older Rogers sisters took it in turn to wash and take back the empty jars and were rewarded with the money to spend on sweeties.

*

Mary Rogers lifted little Betty down from the table and wiped her sticky chin. 'Come on, Bets, let's get your teeth brushed and then you're ready for school.' She led her youngest into the kitchen and stood her on a small stool so that she could reach the taps. Mary sighed as she reached for the tin of dentifrice from the shelf above the sink and took down three toothbrushes from an old jam jar, wishing, not for the first time, that the small terraced house had a bathroom and an inside toilet – known as a carsey in Liverpool – that they didn't have to share with two lots of neighbours. One day, God willing, she was hoping they'd be able to afford something bigger and better, perhaps with a nice backyard of their own. But for now it was enough that she and Harry could keep a roof over their heads and food in their girls' bellies.

Mary laid the brushes on the wooden draining board and spread them with the pink paste. She handed Betty hers and made a brushing motion with her hand up near her mouth to show her what to do. Betty worried her a bit at times as she needed showing the same thing every day.

She'd arrived when Mary had thought she'd done with new babies, and seemed much slower at grasping things than the older two had been. They'd both walked and talked early on and been out of nappies at eighteen months old, even at night. Betty had been nearly four before she'd been dry at night and she'd had to stay in the cot in the same room as Mary and Harry. It wasn't fair to make her share with the older girls.

Bella would have had a fit if Betty's rubber pants had leaked and wet the bed. She was quite fussy, was Bella, very particular in her ways. Always neat and tidy and forever combing her hair. Once Betty was ready to share a bed, she'd gone in with the others and she and Harry had the bedroom to themselves for the first time in years.

Betty finished her tooth-brushing and smiled, baring her teeth for inspection.

'Good girl,' Mary said, rubbing the damp flannel over her chin to wipe off the pink foam that had dribbled down. 'Go and tell Molly and our Bella to come and do theirs and put your wellies on and then I'll take you out the back to the carsey.'

Betty ran off and Mary swilled the sink ready for the other two. Then she pushed her feet into Bella's wellies, opened the back door and peered out, just in time to see their next-door neighbour struggling through the snow in a pair of old boots with no laces. He was making his way up the yard towards the row of carseys with a newspaper under one arm and a packet of fags in his hand. She tutted. He shared with them and he'd be in there all blooming morning. No one else to think about but himself.

'Ken,' she shouted. 'Can you please let the girls use it first? They'll be late for school otherwise and I've got to set off for work shortly.'

Ken Arkness turned around and glared at her. 'I suppose so,' he grumbled. 'But tell 'em to be quick. I had a bad fish from the chippy last night and me stomach's on the turn. Don't know how long I can hold on.' He shuffled back indoors, still grumbling.

Mary shook her head as she led Betty across the yard, lifting her up so that she didn't slip on the icy cobbles. 'Bad fish, my eye,' she muttered. 'More like a bad pint or five.' Thanks God she'd caught him in time as the girls wouldn't set foot in the carsey for ages after he'd been in, and she couldn't blame them.

She yanked on the chain above the toilet as soon as she and Betty had finished. No water flushed out of the cistern. 'I don't believe it,' she groaned. 'Frozen solid.' *Why didn't Harry say anything before he left for work?* Mind you, thinking about it, he hadn't gone outside; he'd just used the chamber pot under the bed as soon as he got up. She'd have to find the little paraffin stove that came out each winter to help thaw the cistern. She hoped there was some paraffin left in it.

Back indoors, and after telling her older two to use the carsey quickly and not to worry about the flushing, Mary rooted in the cupboard under the stairs and found the paraffin lamp. She filled the bowl in the kitchen sink with hot water from the kettle, dropped some pine-scented disinfectant in it and hurried out to the toilet block again, telling Molly to carry the lamp and a box of matches. Mary poured the hot water into the toilet bowl and lit the lamp. She placed it as far back as she could in the small brick-built cubicle.

'That should help, but we need more paraffin for later. I'll get some before I pick up Betty from school,' she told Molly. 'I'd better warn Ken next door so that he doesn't drop his newspaper on the lamp and set the blooming place on fire.'

She hammered on her neighbour's door but there was no reply. Ken was a bit deaf, so Mary tried the handle and stuck her head inside the kitchen, wrinkling her nose at the fetid stench of stale food, grease and an unwashed body. There were dirty pots littering every surface.

'Ken,' she called, 'the carsey's all yours now but be careful as I've had to put a lamp in there, the cistern is frozen up. I've put some hot water down the bowl so it's clean, but if it won't flush for you, I suggest you do the same after you've been.' She paused for breath. 'Get a bucket of hot water and add some bleach or disinfectant to it to freshen it up.'

She hid her irritation as he grumbled that washing carseys was women's work and he'd be doing no such thing. God he was such an awkward bugger, she thought as she went back into her own house. No wonder his wife had run off with the rag and bone man years ago and taken their two kids with her.

Ken wasn't even that old – he'd be younger than Mary's own late dad – but he acted and looked old to get sympathy from the neighbours. Well he was getting none from her today, and with a bit of luck Flo on the other side of him might sort the cleaning out when she came out for her turn to use the carsey. It was an unspoken agreement that Mary and her daughters were first in the morning queue as they all had to leave the house early, while Flo and Ken were at home all day.

'Right, I'm off,' Mary called from down the narrow hall as she buttoned up her coat, pulled off Bella's wellies and slipped on her black zip-up boots over a pair of Harry's old patched-up work socks. Not very glamorous, but she'd take them off when she got to the hospital. For now they'd help prevent her poor old toes from getting chilblains.

'I'll see you all later. Now, Betty, don't you let go of our Bella's hand, and no cutting across The Mystery today because the snow will be deeper on there; stay on the pavements while you get to school.' She fastened a red woollen headscarf over her blonde curly hair and pulled on a pair of matching red mittens. 'Make sure you all put your scarves and hats on. Betty's mittens are in each of her pockets. Enjoy your day, girls.'

'Bye, Mam,' they chorused. Mary closed the front door and walked tentatively down Victory Street to the corner, gasping as a blast of cold air took her breath away. She waved at her friend and workmate Ethel Hardy, who was slowly making her way up Grosvenor Road.

'Morning, Et, here, give us your arm,' Mary greeted her.

'Morning, Mary,' Ethel responded. 'I could have stopped in bed this morning; I can't be doing with this sort of weather.' The pair linked arms and slipped and slithered their way towards the Olive Mount children's hospital to begin their working day.

Chapter Two

Fifteen-year-old Edith Potts made her way slowly from her home on Bligh Street and turned onto Banner Street, which ran parallel. She trod cautiously on the hard-packed snow that covered the icy pavements, terrified of falling. Last winter she'd broken her left wrist and a bone in her lower arm after slipping on ice in the school playground. It had been so painful, taking ages to get right, and this year she was taking no chances. She knocked on the door of number sixteen, a bay-windowed terrace identical to the rest of the street of tightly packed houses, and stood back as someone inside yelled, 'Front door.'

'I'll gerrit,' another voice answered. Footsteps pounded down the hall and the door was flung open by a small boy with freckles and red curly hair that stood out at all angles as though waiting to be tamed with a brush. 'Hiya, Edie,' he said, giving her a gap-toothed smile. 'It's for you, our Fran,' he called over his shoulder. 'It's yer mate. You'd better come in before me mam moans we're letting all the heat out.'

'Thank you, Alfie.' Edie followed the youngest Jackson boy down the narrow hallway and into the back sitting room, where a crackling fire burned in the grate, throwing out welcome warmth.

'Morning, chuck,' Vera Jackson said. 'Park yourself on the sofa while our Fran finishes getting ready. Bit nippy out there this morning.'

'It is,' Edie agreed. 'Bitter cold.' She sat down on the sofa and smiled at the elderly grey-haired lady sitting in a rocking chair by the side of the cast iron fireplace.

The lady smiled back. 'Are you one of ours, chuck?' she asked, looking puzzled. 'You've got blonde hair and ours are all redheads.'

'Mam, she's Doris Potts's daughter,' Vera told her, rolling her eyes behind her mother-in-law's back. 'For the umpteenth time,' she muttered.

'Oh, are you?' Grandma Jackson smiled. 'And how is Doris keeping these days? I was so sorry to hear about your dad, love. Give my condolences to your mam.'

Edie nodded her head and tucked a straying blonde curl back under her woolly hat. 'I will; thank you. And Mam's doing fine, thanks.' The same scene played out most mornings in the Jackson sitting room and within the hour Grandma Jackson had always forgotten all about it. Edie's dad had been dead nearly three years now, following an accident down at the docks where he'd worked with Fran's dad Bert and the two older Jackson boys, Philip and Donald. Thankfully the others had been fine.

Edie always knocked on for Fran each morning. Then they met up with their friend Bella Rogers and her sisters on the corner of Grosvenor Street, and all walked to school together. Monday mornings were a good time for catching up on each other's gossip. Although they'd seen one another at church yesterday, there hadn't been much time to chat. By the time they'd sung in the choir and the service was over, it was time to get home for Sunday dinner. Her mam didn't like to be out too long as her late dad's father, Granddad Potts, couldn't be left for more than a couple of hours on his own in case he wandered off.

By the time Fran put in an appearance it was almost quarter to nine and if they didn't get a move on they'd be late. Today was not a day for running or cutting across The Mystery playground to save time and Edie looked down at her watch, feeling worried.

'Ready when you are,' Fran said, picking up her satchel and looping it around her arms. She shuffled it into place on her back and pecked her mam on the cheek. 'See you later, Mam. Bye, Granny.' She dropped a kiss on top of the old lady's head.

'Edie's been waiting ages,' Vera said, shaking her head. 'God knows what takes you so long, lady. I see you've been curling your hair again. Anyway, it looks nice.'

Fran flicked her auburn waves into place and grinned, her green eyes twinkling. 'Well one never knows who one might meet on the walk to school, does one?' she said in an affected accent with no trace of Liverpudlian at all.

'That's a perfect imitation of Fenella Harrison, if ever I heard one,' Vera Jackson said, looking amused.

'Really, Mother?' Fran raised an eyebrow. 'I can talk posh when the fancy takes me. And if and when Bobby Harrison asks me to be his wife, I'll need to have certain airs and graces to match his mam's.'

'Get away with you. You and your bloody Bobby Harrison. I've seen all you girls making eyes at him after church! Oh, Edie, by the way, will you tell your mam that they've started a meeting group for the likes of Grandma here and your granddad at the church hall. They'll have a cuppa and a bit of a singsong and a game of whist. It's to be held on a Wednesday afternoon starting next week. So if she fancies going with your granddad, I'll take Bert's mam along and me and Doris can have a bit of a break in another part of the hall while the older ones are looked after. Be a nice change for us both.'

Edie smiled and nodded. 'Mam will enjoy that. He drives her mad at times.'

Mrs Jackson winked. 'I know how that feels, chuck. I get fed up to the back teeth of repeating myself over and again. I know they can't help it, but sometimes… This living to a ripe old age is all very well if you've still got your marbles. See you later, gels. Take care out there.'

*

Bella stamped her feet to stop her toes freezing while she waited for her friends Fran and Edie to come into view. She wiped Betty's nose and sighed loudly as Molly rolled a snowball in her gloved hands and chucked it across at two lads who were messing about pushing a large ball of snow in front of them, leaving a slippery path in their wake.

'Where youse going with that?' Molly yelled across the street.

'The Mystery to make a snowman, this is his body. Youse comin' with us, Mol?' the tallest of the pair yelled back.

'No, she's not,' Bella called out. 'The snow will have drifted on there and it will be too deep. We're staying on the streets today.' She spotted her friends coming around the corner of Grosvenor Road and waved. 'And your gloves are gonna be wet through by the time we get to school, so no more making snowballs,' she said to Molly.

'I'll put them on the warm pipes down near me feet,' Molly replied, looking wistfully after the boys as they disappeared from sight around the corner at the top of the street.

'Morning, Fran, Edie,' Bella greeted her pals and fell into step with them, pulling Betty alongside her as Molly followed, grumbling to herself about it not being fair and never having any fun. 'Stop moaning,' Bella said over her shoulder. 'You know what Mam said.'

Edie raised an eyebrow in Molly's direction. 'What's up with you, our kid?'

'Our Bella won't let me go across The Mystery to school.'

Edie shook her head. 'You're best sticking to the footpaths while it's snowing. The Mystery is lovely when the weather's nice, but not today, Mol.'

The girls crossed over Wellington Road and made their way alongside The Mystery park, which had been gifted to the area of Wavertree by an anonymous well-wisher in 1895, earning it its name. The one-hundred-and-four-acre park was popular with the community and provided a safe place for children to play and families to spend their summer weekends. It was also used by cricket and football teams.

The boys who Molly had spoken to had met up with their pals and were building a snowman. Bella shook her head. *Silly lads.* By the time they got into school they'd be wet through and freezing cold and have to sit with wet socks on all day. The Wavertree Church of England school, in a building known as Rose Villas, wasn't the warmest, with its ancient coke boiler that fed the pipes at floor level plus several radiators throughout the building. The system was always breaking down and at this time of year there were often leaks and wet floors to contend with.

As the girls hurried into the school playground, Edie nudged Bella and nodded towards the large front doors, which were being opened. 'Here we go,' Edie said as the hand bell summoning them all to get into their class line-ups rang out. 'Hurry up everyone. The sooner we get inside today, the better.'

But Bella stopped as a tall blond boy ran into the playground with a couple of other lads and joined their class line. She smiled at the boy, who waved and nodded at the three friends.

Handsome Bobby Harrison winked at Bella, who felt her cheeks heating and turned away, making sure that Betty had gone to the right line-up.

Mr Flynn, the teacher in charge of the bell-ringing, cast his stern eye over the stragglers who were running into the playground at the last minute. 'Get a move on,' he shouted. He stood back to let the youngest children in first. Bella waved to Molly, who was leading her class line-up, and smiled reassuringly at little Betty, who always looked so worried as she went into school.

When registration had been called it was Bella's job to take her class register to the head's office before the morning assembly for the older pupils. She hurried into the hall where the top three classes were ready and waiting, and took her place at the front with the rest of the school choir. Bobby Harrison swapped places with his friend so that he was standing next to Bella and winked at her. She smiled shyly at him as the headmaster read out his agenda for the week and then asked the choir members to please step forward. Fran was also in the choir and moved forward so that she was now in between Bobby and Bella, who felt a little surge of jealousy run through her. She knew Fran really liked Bobby but he always seemed to favour Bella over Fran.

Bobby's mother was what Mam called posh. They lived on the well-heeled Prince Alfred Road in a large three-storey Georgian house. 'All them rooms,' Mam had grumbled, 'and her with only one kiddie as well. Such a waste when we're struggling here.' His mother, Fenella, was in charge of running the WI at church and always called him Robert. Mam said she was such a snob and thought herself a cut above everyone else.

But Mam also knew she had a secret past as she'd gone to school with her. A fact Fenella Harrison chose to ignore. Her real name was Elsie Carter and she was from a big, well-known family of crooks from the Old Swan area. She'd changed her name after she met Robert's father and eventually married him. Robert was a nice boy, shy, but then so was Bella. That was probably why they got on so well.

Mr Sykes, the head, raised his baton as Miss May, the music teacher, played the opening chords of 'Jerusalem' on the piano. Bella loved this song. It was so uplifting and always made her feel cheerful for the rest of the day. She wasn't looking forward to the next month, when she would be fifteen and leaving the sanctuary of school and looking for a job.

She'd love to do something nice, go to a college and learn how to use a typewriter so she could work in an office or in a library. Bella loved to read, and to work with books all day would be a pleasant way to earn a living. She could wear smart suits and blouses like the

ladies who worked in Wavertree library, all neat and tidy with their
hair pinned up, instead of pinnies and turbans like most of the mams
she knew wore for work. But she'd need qualifications to become a
librarian and there was little chance of that happening. Her mam
needed her to earn a living to help the family's finances. Her voice
soared above the rest of the choir as she sang a descant, only to be
equalled by Bobby's, blending in perfect harmony. He glanced at her
out of the corner of his eye and smiled, lifting her spirits even further.

Mr Sykes peered at his pupils over the top of his half-frame
glasses and cleared his throat. 'Thank you, choir. That was indeed
a fine performance. You will do us proud at our Easter end-of-term
service next month. Now before they attend morning classes, I'd
like Robert Harrison and Annabelle Rogers to report to my office
in five minutes' time, please. The rest of you, make your way
QUIETLY back to your classrooms.'

'Oooh, what have you two been up to?' Fran said in an exag-
gerated whisper as they left the draughty assembly hall and spilled
out into the main corridor, which always had a smell of carbolic
soap from the nearby cloakrooms, as well as damp.

'Nothing,' Bella replied, frowning. 'Not sure what this is all
about.' She looked at Bobby as the rest of the pupils hurried away.

He shrugged, looking puzzled. 'No idea. But come on, let's
go and see.' He led the way as Bella tried to keep up with his
long strides. They each took a seat outside Mr Sykes's office, Bella
chewing her lips while Bobby gazed around him, seemingly miles
away. The last she'd seen of the headmaster was him talking to Miss
May as the pupils left the hall. He wouldn't be long now.

Mr Sykes appeared around the corner, a sheaf of papers in his
arms. 'Won't be a minute,' he told them. 'My secretary will call
you in shortly.'

As he vanished from sight, Bobby blew out his cheeks and
smiled at Bella. Within seconds the office door flew open and Miss
Scarlett, the head's young secretary, appeared.

'Follow me.' She beckoned to the pair and they followed her into the confines of Mr Sykes's office. His desk was beneath a long window at the top end of the room and Miss Scarlett pointed to two wooden chairs that had been positioned in front of it. 'Take a seat.' She went back to her desk as Mr Sykes leaned forwards, his elbows on the desk and his fingers placed in a steeple in front of him.

'Now there's no need to look so worried,' he said, his blue eyes twinkling. 'It's all good news, well we at the school think so anyway.'

Bobby raised an eyebrow in Bella's direction and then turned his attention back to the headmaster.

'I'm sure you are aware that the scheme known as the Maia Choir performs in various halls, institutes, theatres and churches up and down the country as well as doing the occasional live wireless broadcast,' Mr Sykes began. 'During the recent Christmas period one of their representatives attended a service in our own St Mary's Church and was most impressed with the school choir, particularly the pair of you. Afterwards he attended a meeting of the powers that be and would like to award you both with a scholarship to join the local branch of the Maia Choir.'

Bobby and Bella exchanged surprised grins.

Mr Sykes continued. 'There are two evening classes a week while you train, and eventually you will be placed with a full-time choir and accompanying orchestra to perform all over the country. This opportunity doesn't come around very often and could eventually lead to a really good career for the pair of you.' He sat back, a benevolent smile lighting up his pleasant face.

Bella stared at him, her mouth dropping open. 'Well, I never expected that,' she gasped. 'Oh, I would love to be taught to sing properly. But I'll be starting work next month and I don't know what my mam will say.'

'And I'm supposed to be staying in education to do my school certificates so I can join the air force like my father did, when I'm old enough,' Bobby said. 'But for the time being I'd love to sing more often than I get the chance to. I'll talk to my parents later and see what they think.'

My Sykes smiled and got to his feet. 'I'm sure you'll both do well, but we'll have to see what transpires. Now off you go to class and if your parents need to discuss anything with me they can call the school. Oh, and by the way, keep this to yourselves until we know that you are going to accept the offer. Then we'll announce the news in assembly at the end of the week.'

On the way to their classroom Bella sighed and shook her head. 'Can't see my mam agreeing to this somehow, but I'll ask. Bet yours says it's all right though.'

'We'll see. Be really nice though, Bella. The training place will be somewhere local and I can walk you there and make sure you get home safely. Or my dad will drive us. Be lovely to spend a bit of time together doing something we both enjoy, don't you agree?'

Bella nodded, feeling her cheeks going hot. It definitely would, but what would Fran say when the news came out?

Chapter Three

'And what will it all cost?' Mary asked, draining potatoes over the sink and banging the pan down on the wooden draining board.

Bella frowned and shook her head. 'I don't think it costs anything. Mr Sykes didn't say it did. It's a scholarship, like. They teach us to sing and in time we go out to places with an orchestra and earn a living, I suppose.'

Mary sighed and dropped a lump of margarine in the pan along with a dash of milk. 'Turn them sausages for me,' she said, pointing to the grill pan. 'And you say it's only you and Bobby Harrison that's been asked to do this singing?'

'Yes, Mam. It's a lovely thing to happen and you know how much I like to sing.'

Mary looked at her eldest's face. It was alight with joy and her eyes were shining. *But that might have more to do with Bobby than the singing*, she thought, and then cursed herself for thinking so cynically. She half-smiled and started to mash the potatoes with the end of her wooden rolling pin. She should feel proud that her girl, and that bloody Elsie Carter's son, would be taking singing lessons together. 'Hmm, well we'll have to see what your dad says when he gets home. You'll be looking for a job in a few weeks and you might have to do shifts and not be available at night.'

Bella nodded. 'I know that. But I could do it until then and see how it goes. If I get a job where I just work in the day I can still have the singing lessons.'

'Set the table and we'll talk about it when we've had our tea,' Mary said, dismissing the subject. She shook her head as Bella left the kitchen. If only the family didn't need an extra wage coming in it would be fine and a great opportunity for her daughter, who was always such a good help to her. But times were hard and every penny counted. Not many kids from the back streets of Wavertree got the opportunity to do anything as nice as that. She and Harry would have to put their heads together later and have a good think about it.

*

After tea Bella sat on the big double bed and got Betty ready for bed. She'd brought a bowl of warm water and some soap and a flannel up with her and had given her little sister a strip wash, brushed her hair and re-plaited it. Betty was almost asleep as Bella slipped her winceyette nightdress over her head and tucked her under the blankets.

Molly was next door at her friends' for half an hour and Bella could hear the soft murmur of voices downstairs as her mam and dad sat talking in front of the fire after their meal. She wondered if they'd come to a decision about the singing lessons yet. On the walk home from school she'd been dying to say something to Fran and Edie, but had kept quiet as per Mr Sykes's instructions.

She knew that Fran really liked Bobby and the idea that Bella would get to spend more time in his company would annoy her. But Bella also liked him and he seemed to like her. If it came to a choice between Bobby and Fran, though, Bella knew that her loyalties would have to be to her friend – but would Fran do the same for her?

She left the room, closing the door quietly behind her. Downstairs, Mam smiled as she walked into the sitting room.

'Come and sit down, chuck,' she said, indicating the seat next to her on the sofa. Dad was seated in his old armchair by the fire, the *Liverpool Echo* newspaper on the floor by his feet.

Bella joined her mam. Her stomach was churning, but they looked relaxed and happy enough.

'Now then,' Dad began. 'Your mam's explained about the singing lessons and I gather you'd like to give it a go.'

Bella nodded, crossing her fingers in her lap. 'I would, Dad.'

'So if we say it's all right, and you manage to get a job that fits in, then we'd be happy for you. Let's see how the next few weeks pan out, shall we? But for now, the answer is yes. We do need you to be working for a living, gel, when you leave school. You understand that, don't you?'

Bella nodded. 'Yes, of course I do. And I will. We've got a man coming in to speak to us about jobs and stuff and how to apply for them soon. I'm sure there will be something for me.'

Her mam patted her hand. 'Enjoy it while you can, love, the singing I mean.'

On Tuesday morning Bella was hanging her coat on a peg in the school cloakroom when Bobby caught up with her. She'd hung back as Edie and Fran had dashed away towards the classroom, hoping Bobby would hurry up and show his face.

'Any luck?' he whispered.

Bella looked around to make sure no one was eavesdropping. 'Yes. They said it's okay, well at least until I start work and then we'll have to see.'

'That's great. We'll go to the head's office at first break then and let him know. I'll leave class first and then meet you at the top of the corridor so that no one realises we're on a mission.'

'Okay.' Bella picked up her satchel and made her way to the classroom. Halfway through the first lesson she was conscious of Fran looking at her. She half-smiled and tried to concentrate on the geography lesson but her mind was all over the place.

'What's up with you?' Fran hissed as the teacher, Mr Gutteridge, turned and pointed to a map of Europe pinned on the blackboard. 'You're miles away and you've got a soppy look on your face.'

'Nothing,' Bella hissed back. 'And I have not got a soppy look on my face.'

'Sorry.' Fran rolled her eyes and stuck out her lower lip in a pretend pout.

When the first break bell rang out, Bella made the excuse that she needed the toilet and dashed out ahead of her friends. She hung back near the cloakroom, ducking behind rows of coats, until they'd gone past towards the playground. She stuck her head out and spotted Bobby waiting for her. He grinned and waved and the pair hurried to Mr Sykes's office and Bobby rapped on the door. Miss Scarlett let them in.

'Take a seat,' she said. 'Mr Sykes has just gone to visit a class-room. He won't be a moment.'

Mr Sykes dashed back into his office and beckoned them to follow him to his desk. He looked at them expectantly as Bella began, her words tumbling over one another.

'Yes, er, yes, we are going to accept the scholarships.'

'We are indeed,' Bobby agreed.

'Well that's marvellous news,' Mr Sykes said, beaming. 'I will let them know. They'll be in touch soon with details and we'll take it from there. I'll make an announcement during Friday morning's assembly. Just keep it to yourselves for the next few days.'

On Friday morning before the pupils were dismissed from assem-bly to make their way to their classrooms, Mr Sykes called Bella and Bobby to the front of the hall. With a smile on his face, he announced the good news of their Maia Choir scholarships and everyone in the room applauded. Everyone, Bella noticed, except Fran, who stared at her with a stony-faced expression. Next to Fran, Edie gave an encouraging little wave and carried on clapping.

Bella sighed inwardly. Why couldn't her friend be happy for her? She knew that sulky face wasn't anything to do with the singing, because Fran was never that bothered about it, despite also being in the church choir. It was all to do with her spending time with Bobby. Bella took a deep breath and went to join her classmates, who patted her on the back and wished her well, as did Bobby's friends to him over the other side of the hall.

During break time the three girls huddled together under the bike shelter. It was still cold but the snow was beginning to melt. Fran ignored her while Bella chatted to Edie about this and that, anything rather than bring up the subject of singing.

'So when do you start the lessons?' Fran interrupted, surprising Bella.

'Er, next Tuesday I think. It's just two evenings a week for now in the church hall.'

'And I suppose Bobby will walk you there and back, will he?'

'Oh, I don't know. That's not been decided yet,' Bella answered as lightly as she could.

'You know how much I like him,' Fran spat.

'Yes,' Bella replied. 'And I'm sure he likes you too. We're only singing, you know, it's nothing else.'

'Give it time.'

Bella and Edie stared as Fran stomped away from them. 'I'm sorry she's being like this, Bella,' Edie said. 'She's jealous. She knows that Bobby never looks at her like he looks at you.'

Bella shrugged, feeling her cheeks heating at the thought of Bobby looking at her in any special sort of way. 'I don't want to fall out with her over this. And it might only be for a few weeks. I'll be working soon and might not have the time. I just want to enjoy it while I can and Bobby feels the same.'

The bell for end of break time rang out and Edie linked her arm through Bella's as they made their way indoors. There was no sign of Fran until they got inside the classroom, where she was already sitting at her desk, her arms folded and a mutinous expression on her face. Bella's heart sank as she sat down beside her. She really didn't want to fall out with her lifelong friend over this, but unless Fran was willing to talk to her, there wasn't much else she could do.

Chapter Four

March 1939

On Tuesday, the day before Bella's fifteenth birthday, Bobby called for her to walk to the church hall for their singing lesson. This was their third week and both were enjoying the challenge. They'd fitted in well with the rest of the Maia Choir in the group they'd been assigned to and last Thursday the leader had told them how very pleased he was with their progress so far.

Bella was thrilled, but Fran had still not spoken to her properly since the announcement in the assembly hall and she felt hurt that her friend couldn't be happy for her. Mam said it was because Fran had always had her own way, being the only girl in the family, and she'd been spoiled, Bella shouldn't let it bother her. Edie had said the same. But it did bother her. After the Easter holiday next week all three would be starting work at the match factory in the packing department and she'd rather the air be cleared between them before then.

Bryant & May's match factory in Garston was a bit of a trek at nearly four miles but there wasn't a lot of choice. The tram or train would take them there if no one could offer a lift. The days would be long and it would be difficult to get home in time for her singing lessons. Tate and Lyle's had no vacancies and nor did

Littlewood's Pools or Hartley's, which were all a bit closer to home. There were no nice office jobs around that didn't require typing qualifications and a bit of further education, but that was out of the question for Bella. It was their final day in school on Thursday. Next week Bobby was starting at the Liverpool Mechanics' School of Arts to continue his education until he was old enough to be recruited into the RAF. Bella envied him and wished she could have the same opportunities.

She smiled as she let him in while she put on her coat. 'Bye everyone,' she called as they left the house.

She and Bobby walked along the street in silence, Bella swinging her small black handbag with her key and purse tucked inside. She could have put them in her coat pocket but she felt the bag was a nice touch and most of the girls in the choir carried a small handbag, so she'd dug out an old one of Mam's from the bottom of the wardrobe and cleaned it up a bit. With a little silk scarf tucked around her neck, it made her feel a bit more grown up.

'Are you looking forward to your birthday tomorrow?' Bobby asked, breaking the silence.

'Yes, I am. Mam's doing a little tea party after school for the family. We always do that for each one of us. Why don't you call in for a slice of cake?' She invited him before she could stop herself, then felt really embarrassed as he paused walking. She was so relieved when he looked at her, a big grin splitting his face.

'I'd love to. What time?'

'Oh, er, well about half past five. Is that okay?'

'Of course. Thank you. I'll look forward to it.'

Bella took a deep breath as they walked into the church hall. Why had she done that? Edie was going to call in for cake and she'd invited Fran on the way home from school the other day. Her invite had been snubbed, but what if Fran did decide to turn up? She'd think Bella was rubbing her nose in it on purpose when Bobby arrived too. She couldn't un-invite him now as that would look rude.

She'd just have to pray Fran didn't come round. It was all mixed up because she'd really like Fran to be at her birthday tea so they could be good friends again. Oh why was life so complicated at times?

Bella and Bobby were greeted by the other choir members, who were hanging their coats in the cloakroom and making their way into the wide hall. They took their seats and the pianist sat down and shuffled through her music case. She took out a book, opened it and placed it on the piano's music stand. The leader picked up his baton and they started with a few hymns and then moved onto modern songs that were popular at the moment.

When Bella was asked to take a solo lead in 'Over the Rainbow' she felt sure her throat would seize up and choke her, but the lovely melody carried her through and the others sang along with her, filling the room with their beautiful harmonies. She felt quite broken when the song finished, but the leader clapped and smiled at her. 'Bravo,' he mouthed, filling her with pride.

They took a break at that point and a lady with a steel urn on a trolley pushed it into the room and proceeded to pour mugs of steaming tea. 'I was stood near the door when you was singing, gel,' she said to Bella. 'And the 'airs on me neck stood on end. It were really beautiful. You'll go far with a voice like that, queen.'

Bella thanked her and took a seat beside Bobby. 'I wish,' she said quietly.

'You wish what?' he said, his head on one side.

'Well, what that tea lady said, that I could go far with my voice, which would be much nicer than packing matches into boxes for a living.'

He smiled and squeezed her hand. 'Bella, you may well do just that. None of us know what the future holds. I know you have to start at the matchworks after the Easter weekend, but if you try your hardest to get here in time for the lesson, both of us that is, and we work as hard as we can, you never know. It's a chance of a lifetime and we have to try and make it work.'

She nodded and finished her tea, hoping with all her heart that he was right.

Bella had just blown out the candles on the birthday cake that Mam had made her when Molly said she'd heard a knock at the door. They'd almost missed it, with them all singing 'Happy Birthday to You'. 'I'll get it,' Molly yelled, shooting out of the back sitting room.

'It's your friend Bobby,' she announced, leading him into the room.

Bobby smiled as all eyes turned to him. He held out a parcel wrapped in pink paper and a white envelope. 'Happy birthday, Bella,' he said, handing them over to her.

'Thank you.' Bella smiled. 'I'll open it with my other presents when Dad comes home from work. He's on a late shift today. Have a seat next to Edie.' She felt herself gabbling and gestured to the sofa. 'I'll get you a cup of tea; unless you'd rather have orange squash.' She pointed to the glass jug on the table. 'It's a bit watered down though,' she whispered finally.

'Tea would be lovely,' he said.

'I'll get Edie another cup too.' Bella dashed into the kitchen, where a freshly brewed pot of tea stood on the small countertop. Fancy Bobby getting her a present. She hadn't been expecting that. In fact, she'd half thought he'd change his mind and wouldn't come. Edie had already told her that Fran wasn't coming, but she'd sent a birthday card with Edie after ignoring Bella all day in school. That didn't make sense really. She hadn't read it yet as she had put it with the others to wait until Dad got home later.

Mam was cutting up the cake and handed slices round on small plates to Bobby and Edie. 'What a shame we haven't got a piano,' she said. 'You and our Bella could have given us a song.'

Bobby laughed. 'I should have brought my squeezebox. But I suppose we still could. That's if Bella would like to.' He raised an eyebrow at her as she came into the room with a tray of cups.

'Oh, I don't know,' Bella began. 'We need accompaniment.'

'Comb and paper,' suggested Molly. 'I know how to play that new "Jeepers Creepers" song.'

Bella laughed. 'Go on then. Let Bobby have his cake and brew first. Edie can sing as well so she can harmonise with us.'

Molly dashed upstairs to find a comb, and got some tissue paper from under the kitchen sink.

'Don't you be wasting that toilet paper,' Mam warned. 'It's Izal that, and it's not cheap. One sheet only, Molly.' She collected up the plates and cups and took then through to the kitchen while Molly did a few practices on her comb and paper instrument.

Bobby counted them in and he and Bella got to their feet and sang a rousing version of 'Jeepers Creepers', Edie joining in occasionally and Bella opening her eyes wide to stare into Bobby's blue ones. When they'd finished a cheer went up and everyone clapped.

'You three are dead good,' Molly said. 'What else do you know? You're like the singers in some of the films I've seen.'

'Oh, that reminds me,' Mam said. 'My workmate Ethel Hardy told me that new Abbey picture house on Church Road is lovely. It opened the other week and she went last Saturday night.'

'Oh,' Bella said, sitting down next to Edie. 'We'll have to see what's on.'

'Shall we have a go at "Thanks for the Memory"? Bobby suggested. 'Can you play that, Molly?'

'Yes, I can.' She gave a little blast on her comb and Bobby started to sing, pulling Bella back onto her feet. They harmonised together, looking into each other's eyes again.

'Sing the rainbow song,' Betty said, her eyes shining. 'I like that.'

'Okay, just for you then, Betty,' Bobby said, smiling at the little girl, who clapped her hands as they began.

'You're really good, you two,' Edie said as they finished. She got to her feet. 'It's no surprise you won that scholarship. And those lessons are paying off well. I can see you onstage at a theatre in time.'

'Thank you, Edie, you're a gem,' said Bella. 'But you're good too. It was so fun to sing together.'

The girls smiled at each other and Edie came over to give Bella a hug. ' Right, I'm going to get off now so I can help Mam with me granddad. He gets a bit cantankerous around teatime. She says she thinks it's when he's hungry and it plays havoc with his system. Whatever that means.' She rolled her eyes. 'Thanks very much for the sandwiches and cake, Mrs Rogers. I'll see you tomorrow, Bella. Last day of being schoolgirls for us. Sad in a way, isn't it? But still we'll be working girls next week and bringing in a wage.'

Bobby smiled. 'I'd better get off as well. My godfather is visiting tonight and Mother said I should be there. Thank you very much for the invite to tea. I'll see you tomorrow, Bella.'

Bella showed her guests out and waved them off down the street, watching as Edie went one way at the end and Bobby went the other. He turned and waved one last time and then vanished from sight. Bella shut the door and leaned against it, smiling. That had been a lovely hour. She couldn't wait for her dad to get home now and then, when he'd had his tea, she could open her presents.

Bella sat by the fire and watched her dad wolfing down a plate of scouse, dunking bread into the last of the gravy. He sat back with a satisfied sigh. 'I needed that. Right then, come on, gel. I know you've waited patiently for me and you must be dying to know what's in them parcels.' He pointed to the small pile of gifts at the end of the table.

Bella smiled and opened her mam and dad's parcel first. Inside was a black wool skirt with a kick-pleat at the back and a neat white cotton blouse with pearl buttons down the front and on the cuffs of the long sleeves. Mam looked pleased as Bella exclaimed that they were lovely.

'I thought you could do with a nice smart outfit for when you do the singing. I saw a picture of a Maia Choir and the ladies all seemed to be wearing something similar.'

'They do at that, Mam. Thank you. Those are really nice.' She opened Edie's gift of lavender-scented bath cubes and matching talc next, and then Bobby's parcel last. She smiled as she saw the Dairy Box milk chocolates inside. She'd never had a box of chocolates before, never even seen one close to, just on the shelf in shops.

'Oh you lucky girl,' her mam exclaimed. 'And you know what the advert says don't you? "She'll love you if they're Dairy Box."'

Bella felt her cheeks warming. 'Mam, don't be so daft. But I'm really going to enjoy these. What a treat. I'll share them with you all at the weekend, seeing as it's Easter.'

'We'll look forward to that, queen,' Dad said, giving her a hug.

Bella opened her birthday cards and stood them on the mantelpiece. Fran's just said, 'From Fran.' It was better than nothing, she supposed. She peeped at Bobby's written message again, 'To Bella. With love from your friend Bobby.' A little thrill went through her.

*

'What's up?' Mary asked as she heard Harry swearing. Their daughters were all in bed and he was sitting in his favourite chair by the dying embers of the fire with his feet up while she made them some cocoa in the kitchen. She popped her head around the doorway. He was waving his evening *Echo* in the air and pointing at the headline. 'What is it?'

'That bastard Hitler,' he said, shaking his head. 'He's only gone and violated the Munich Agreement.'

'What does that mean?' Mary asked, coming into the room. Harry looked worried and a little shiver of fear ran down her spine.

'Well he wants European domination and he's evil enough to try and get it. You know that ours, Italy, and France's prime ministers, along with Hitler, signed that agreement last September. Neville Chamberlain went over to Munich for the signing.'

Mary nodded. 'I remember. He gave a speech afterwards that went on and on.'

'He did,' Harry agreed. 'But he knows what he's talking about. Anyway, that agreement averted the outbreak of war. Now Hitler is doing his utmost to take over Czechoslovakia to create a greater Germany. Czechoslovakia now wants France and Britain to come to their aid, but Chamberlain's said no. Unfortunately Hitler is now in the throes of making sure the country ceases to exist.'

Mary chewed her lip anxiously. 'Surely he can't do that, can he?'

'He already has done, love. He's ruthless. This isn't looking good, chuck, not good at all.' He sighed. 'Mind you, I think we've all known it's been coming for some time. If you remember, last year in August Chamberlain ordered the Air Raid Precaution wardens to requisition cellars and basements for air raid shelters. Don't you remember when that ARP fellow knocked to ask if we had one? We're lucky ours is dry enough to use, but for anyone without one there's those Anderson shelters that were being given out and many people have got them already in place in their gardens and backyards.'

Mary nodded and pursed her lips. 'Let's not get carried away just yet. It might all blow over.'

Harry shook his head as she went back into the kitchen.

Chapter Five

Friday, 1 September 1939

Bella, Fran and Edie got off the tram outside Bryant & May's, glad to get away from the doom and gloom and uncertainty about Europe that all the passengers were talking about. It was all anyone talked about these days. Although not a lot had happened yet in Liverpool, it was the threat that worried people.

Since starting work in March, and meeting a young match worker who she was now doing a bit of courting with, Fran had apologised to Bella for being 'a right cow over Bobby', as she put it, and the pair were now pals again, although Bella still felt a bit hurt by Fran's earlier jealous behaviour. After all, there was nothing going on romantically between her and Bobby; they were just good friends who sang in the choir and now went to the Abbey picture house occasionally.

He was busy doing extra school stuff and exams ready for joining the air force and she was busy with her job; neither had much spare time for anything else. She linked arms with Edie, glad that today was Friday and also payday. Tomorrow afternoon, the threesome planned to go into the city centre to see what bargains the stalls in Paddy's Market had to offer.

They walked up the wide tree-lined path towards the factory. Bella thought how smart it looked in the morning sunlight. On the roof, the huge cylindrical water tower with its pointed top dominated the two-storey building, just above the Bryant & May sign. Between the white concrete columns, decorated with Lancashire roses, the front was filled with glass that glinted in the light.

She enjoyed working here, in spite of the long hours and it not being quite the job she would have liked. Counting matches and packing them into small boxes was so boring, but the rest of the staff were nice to get along with and had made the new girls welcome. Being on their feet all day took some getting used to after sitting down in school, and blisters on toes and heels were common occurrences.

But after listening to the horrendous tales of bygone days from workers whose match-worker relatives had suffered from a condition called phossy jaw, where the bones of the jaw had literally rotted away, causing severe disfigurement – or death in many cases – there was a lot to be thankful for now the manufacturing process had been changed and white phosphorous was no longer used in the production of matches.

Later that morning, as the packing department took a tea break, one of the foremen from the manufacturing department dashed into the canteen, a grim look on his face. He climbed up on a chair, clapped his hands for their attention and called for quiet. 'We've got the wireless on upstairs,' he began. 'There's just been a news bulletin from London. Hitler and his Nazi cronies have invaded Poland.'

There was silence for a few seconds and then everyone started talking at once. People wanted more details.

'And how does that affect Britain?' a bald man sitting at the next table to Bella and her friends asked.

'I think we'll have to wait for further announcements before we all start panicking,' the foreman replied. 'But at the moment it's not looking good and we need to be prepared.'

Bella took a deep breath. 'I heard my dad telling Mam that if Hitler tried to take over anywhere other than Czechoslovakia there'd definitely be another war.' She shuddered. 'I have to admit it, I'm scared.'

'Me too,' Edie said and Fran nodded her head in agreement, her green eyes wide in her pale face.

Back in the packing department the mood among the workers varied.

'We can't let that bleedin' dictator have all his own way,' one man said. 'We need to show him who's boss.'

'Who's we, Arnie?' another man said. 'I don't wanna be fighting no bloody war; I had enough of that a few years back. Me leg's never been right since. I'm far too old for all that malarkey now.'

'Aye, you and me both,' another man spoke up. 'But then, I don't want my lad to get dragged into it either. He's getting married next month. He won't want that.'

By the end of the shift Bella had heard enough. She couldn't wait to get home, where her dad would surely reassure her that it would all be sorted soon enough and there would be no need for another war. Her mam only spoke occasionally of what had gone on during the First World War, but every now and then she'd stare into space as though remembering things she'd seen and heard. She had been eleven and her dad thirteen when that war broke out. They'd both lost older brothers in combat. Uncles Bella had never met, but they were still remembered. It was all very worrying and she didn't know what to think.

On the wireless that night the prime minister had announced that he would be making a statement on Sunday. Everyone dashed home from the Sunday morning church services. Bella had sung briefly with Bobby, who said he'd see her on Tuesday at choir, all being well.

The family gathered in the sitting room with the wireless turned up full blast; Mam, Molly and Bella sitting at the table clutching mugs of hot tea, while Dad sat near the wireless in his armchair,

Betty on his knee, fiddling with the dial on the Bakelite set to get the best reception he could manage. At eleven fifteen, Mr Chamberlain began his announcement:

> I am speaking to you from the cabinet room at Ten Downing Street. This morning the British ambassador in Berlin handed the German government a final note stating that unless we heard from them by eleven o'clock that they were prepared at once to withdraw their troops from Poland, a state of war would exist between us. I have to tell you now that no such undertaking has been received, and that consequently this country is at war with Germany.

Mam let out a strangled sob and dropped her mug, tea running all over the tablecloth. Bella jumped up and brought a dishcloth through from the kitchen. She mopped up the mess. The prime minister was now talking about various tradesmen who would not be expected to join the troops to fight this war and she heard transport workers mentioned, which meant her dad was safe here for the time being. Mr Chamberlain was also saying that they would need to listen out for instructions over the next few days about what to do and how to help themselves. All they could do was hope and pray that it would soon be over and they could all get back to normal.

It was a subdued threesome that jumped off the tram on Monday morning and headed into Bryant & May's. The journey from home had been fairly quiet as people talked behind their hands in whispers about the fate of Poland. *Bloody Hitler is a monster*, Bella thought, there was no denying it, but surely he'd stop soon.

Mam had spent last night making a list of things to take down the cellar to make it comfortable, just in case, she'd said, so God knows what she was expecting to happen. Dad had added that everyone would need a safe place to shelter in the event of an air raid. Bella hated the cellar; it was full of spiders and mouse droppings and smelled of damp. It was hardly ever used apart from storing coal and her dad's toolbox. The thoughts of having to live down there instead of in the house filled her with dread.

The wireless crackled in the background. Bella caught the mention of Poland as the frequency whistled in and out. Two men with posh accents droned on in conversation as the packers counted the matches and placed them into the small boxes lined up on the workbenches. It seemed everyone was on tenterhooks, anxiously waiting for the next announcement of doom and gloom. They needed something to cheer them all up. Maybe some music. 'Shall we sing?' Bella whispered to Edie.

'Sing? Why?'

'Oh, you know, just to make things feel a bit happier. We all used to join in when a song came on the wireless before all this war stuff began.'

'Okay, why not.' Edie smiled. 'You start and we'll join in.'

Bella cleared her throat and began to sing 'Alexander's Ragtime Band', singing Bing Crosby's part, and Edie and Fran harmonised Connee Boswell's bit .The workers smiled as the girls wiggled their hips and one of the men pretended he was blowing a trumpet. By the time the song ended all the factory floor workers had joined in, including the usually serious-faced foreman. He clapped, as did everyone else, and the girls took a bow.

'Well done, gels. That cheered them all up a bit,' the foreman said. 'You three are dead good. Like them Andrews Sisters. You can give 'em another when you come back from your break.'

'So what else can we sing?' Fran asked. 'Needs to be something a bit jolly that they can join in with. I really enjoyed doing that you know. It was a good idea of yours, Bella.'

'Thanks.' Bella wrapped her hands around her mug of tea. Fran seemed to be softening towards her but there was still a bit of an oddness about her whenever Edie mentioned Bobby and the singing classes, a subject that Bella tried to steer clear of in Fran's presence. It was only on the odd occasion that Edie had asked if she was out at singing practice tonight on their way home from work, but lately she seemed to have realised it was a subject best not spoken about unless she and Bella were alone.

'"Whistle While you Work" is jolly,' Bella said, 'and the men can whistle along for us, and maybe "Apple Blossom Time", we'll see how it goes and how much time we've got.'

The afternoon drifted by. Bella had the workers singing along after the ten-minute break at three thirty, and by the time the hooters sounded at six they were all far more cheerful than they'd been earlier in the day.

Chapter Six

October 1939

By the last week of October things had started to change and the threat of war began to feel a reality to the residents of Liverpool. Rootes factory in Speke, not far from the matchworks, had begun production on Halifax Bombers and shells, in a newly formed munitions department.

Dad had come home and told them that his best mate was leaving his job as a conductor on the trams and going to work at the Royal Ordnance Factory over in Kirkby. It was a case of all hands on deck to manufacture as many bombs, fighter planes and other ammunition as the country could manage. Each city with a port was rumoured to be under threat and Liverpool was a big port with docks and frequent ships carrying and delivering goods and passengers on a daily basis.

Bella arrived home from work on the Friday night to find her mam in tears, sitting at the table with a letter clutched in her hand. 'Mam, what's happened?' She sat down opposite and stared as her mam wiped her eyes on a hanky she pulled from up the sleeve of her sweater.

She handed the letter to Bella, who read through it and looked up. 'Evacuation? What, you might have to let the kids go to strangers?'

Mam nodded. 'I've got to register them as soon as possible in readiness for that programme they mention in the letter.'

'Where are they now?' Bella looked around the empty room. Apart from their school coats over the arm of the sofa there was no sign of her sisters.

'Molly is at her friend's house until we have tea and the little one is asleep on the bed upstairs. She's not well. The teacher said she'd been complaining of a sore throat and was a bit warm to the touch. There's a lot of scarlet fever going round, we've a few in at the hospital at the moment in isolation. I hope she's not coming down with that.'

'Oh Mam, I'm sure it's just a cold starting,' Bella said, trying to reassure her.

'But it's not like her to fall asleep before she's eaten. As if I haven't got enough to worry about right now. Our Molly will go mad if I have to send her away, and Betty, well, I don't think she'd settle anywhere. You know what she's like; she's not the same as others her age. Me and your dad, well, we've always been a bit worried about her.'

'I know, Mam.' Bella reached out for her hand across the table. 'It might not happen though. They may just be doing this as a safety measure, like, you know, just in case.'

Mam shook her head. 'I doubt it. They are putting everything in place. Air raid shelters and gas masks are next and we've been told to get a special tape so we can protect our windows. There's a diagram of how to do it that you get at the shop where you buy the tape from.' She sighed. 'Oh and there's talk of blackouts coming soon as well. You have to make sure there's no light showing from your doors and windows at night so the Germans can't see there are houses and other buildings below when they are flying over.'

Bella swallowed the lump in her throat. Life was changing rapidly, far too quickly for her liking. It was a frightening thought that Germans would be flying over their city looking for places to drop bombs. She'd seen the reports and news at the Abbey picture house, of what had gone on in Poland, terrified people being rounded up like sheep by the German army and herded along the streets to be kept as prisoners or even shot. It didn't bear thinking about.

'Anyway,' Mam continued. 'This weekend I want you to help me get the cellar ready for us sleeping down there. I've got a few things and your dad will give it a clean-out, get rid of the mice and spiders and give the walls a coat of paint to freshen them up a bit. Then we'll make it as cosy as we can. We'll get another paraffin stove to take the chill off. I'm afraid we are all going to have to make the best of things for a while, chuck.'

Bella tried hard not to let her horror show as Mam got to her feet. Every family in the country was probably making the same sort of plans as her mam right now, so they weren't alone, but it was a daunting feeling. Hitler's bombs or spiders; the thought of both put the fear of God in her, equally.

'Have you got a cellar?' she asked Bobby as they walked to the church hall on Tuesday night for the singing lesson. She told him what her family had been doing all weekend in their preparations for the possibility of air raids.

He nodded. 'There's about four under the house. But only one that we could use as the others are full of stuff that's stored down there. My parents have been making arrangements to have it fitted out so that we can sleep there if needs be. But my mother wants us to go and stay in the country with some family friends.'

'And will you go?' Bella hoped he wouldn't. At least with Bobby around she still had someone to go to the choir practice and the pictures with. Edie wasn't coming out much lately other than going to work as her mam was struggling with Granddad Potts, and Fran was seeing as much of her boyfriend Frankie as she could because he'd told her that if they needed more soldiers to fight off the Germans he'd be joining the army. He was a good bit older than Fran was, nearly eighteen, so would be able to sign up as soon as he'd made his decision.

'Not sure. I'd rather stay in the city. I've thought about joining the air force, as you know. Father wants me to wait until I'm eighteen but with this war hanging over us, I might be able to join earlier – or there's the army, I suppose.'

Fran stopped walking and stared at him. 'What, you'd go away and fight? Like maybe to France?'

He shrugged. 'I've no idea. I'd have to wait and see where they'd send me. Mother would have a fit if they sent me abroad, but if the country needs us to do that, then, well, it's what I'd have to do.'

'Oh God, this is horrible.' Bella burst into tears. 'My sisters may have to go away, evacuated, they call it. Mam got a letter today. We all have to be prepared to sleep in the cellar and now you're talking about going away to fight. Dad said Chamberlain was backing down on things as well and we need a better man than him in charge. Why do we have to be dragged into this mess? I thought it would all get sorted out without this happening.'

Bobby put his arms around her and gave her a hug. 'Bella, it's not something that can be sorted out in a hurry. There's a madman intent on capturing the whole of Europe, no matter what. He has to be stopped. And we will all have to pull together on this. Come on, don't cry.' He wiped her eyes with a spotless white handkerchief he pulled from his jacket pocket. 'Let's try and enjoy our singing lesson while we still can.'

*

'But I can't let our little Betty go,' Mary cried. Harry had arrived home from work earlier and she'd let him finish his tea before she'd shown him the evacuation letter. 'No one will understand her like we do. If they shout at her for wetting the bed or because she's struggling to do up her shoes or wipe her nose, she'll never cope. We, as her mam and dad, know she's not like her sisters, Harry. She's always been a bit slow, but we can manage her because we know that. But a stranger won't and they'll think she's being naughty or something.'

She sobbed heartbrokenly and Harry got up from his chair and took her in his arms. He sighed into her hair and held her tight. 'Mary, love, I'm sure if you explain when you register their names, they'll be able to reassure you that Betty will be well taken care of. And if they put our Molly and Bets together then Molly can look after her.'

Mary looked up and wiped her eyes. 'What do you mean – if? There's no if about it. They have to be together. I'm not letting them go unless they can guarantee that and if they can't then I'm going with them.'

Harry nodded. 'I'm sure they will, but you will have to tell the people at the office that Betty needs to be with her big sister. Now come on, sit down and I'll make you a nice cup of tea.'

'I'll just go up and see if she's okay,' Mary said. 'She was really hot when I got her into bed. She's sickening for something, I'm sure.' She hurried out of the room.

'Harry, Harry, come here quick,' she shouted from upstairs. 'I can't wake our Betty up. You'll have to run and fetch the doctor.'

Harry shot up the stairs two at a time. Mary was sitting on the bed cradling little Betty in her arms.

'She's burning up and she's breathing funny,' Mary sobbed.

'I'll go and get the doctor,' Harry said. 'I'll knock on for Molly and get her to come home. Is Bella at her singing lesson?'

'Yes, she is,' Mary wailed. 'She won't be long now.'

*

Harry ran down the stairs and pulled on his cap and jacket, then hurried up the street, calling at Molly's friend's house and telling her to go home right away. He dashed as fast as he could to the old house on Picton Road where Doctor Hope lived and held his surgery. His wife answered the door as Harry gasped that his little daughter was poorly and not waking up.

'Doctor Hope is out on a call, but I'll send him straight round to your house as soon as he gets back,' Mrs Hope told Harry and wrote down his address.

'Thank you,' Harry said and dashed back the way he'd come. Bella was strolling up Grosvenor Road with Bobby as he rounded the corner and he called out to her. 'Our Betty is proper poorly and I've just been for the doctor,' he told her. 'He's coming as soon as he can.'

'You'd better go with your dad,' Bobby said. 'I'll call round tomorrow to see how your sister is. Take care of yourself.'

Bella waved goodbye and linked her arm through her dad's as they hurried towards Victory Street and home.

Molly was in the kitchen filling a bowl with cold water for her mam to sponge Betty down to help cool her a bit. 'Mam said there are some cloths under the sink but I can't find them,' Molly said. 'Do you know where they are?' she asked Bella.

Bella rooted in the cupboard and pulled out some pieces of white muslin, then took the bowl from Molly. 'She'll mean these. I'll take it all up. You stay down here with Dad in case Betty's got something that's catching.'

'Bit late for that seeing as we two shared the bed with her as usual last night,' Molly said, folding her arms.

Bella glared at her sister, who wasn't usually so flippant, and dashed away, calling, 'Make Dad a brew and listen out for the doctor knocking on.'

*

Upstairs Mam was holding Betty, who was limp in her arms. The look of despair in her mam's eyes shocked Bella. She put the bowl on the floor beside the bed.

'She opened her eyes a few minutes ago,' Mam said. 'I checked her throat because she said it hurts. It's all grey, the back of her tongue and her tonsils, the glands in her neck are swollen and she's breathing funny too.'

'That doesn't sound good,' Bella said. 'What do you think it could be?'

'I don't even want to think about it, chuck,' Mam whispered. 'But I've seen a throat like that before and it frightens the life out of me—' She stopped as a loud banging on the front door sounded. Then footsteps pounded the stairs and the doctor came into the room. He put his bag down on the bed and examined Betty, who was now as limp as a rag doll in Mam's arms.

'How long has she been like this, Mary?' he asked, his face serious.

'Since she got in from school, but she's been a bit quiet for the last couple of days, not quite right, you know.'

The doctor nodded. 'I need to admit her to hospital right away. We'll take her to Olive Mount. I know you work there and it's close by. I'll go back to the surgery and get an ambulance on its way. Pack her a small bag and I'll meet you there.' He dashed out of the room and ran down the stairs.

*

Harry was waiting at the bottom of the stairs. Before he'd even had a chance to open his mouth the doctor shook his head. 'I'm almost certain it's diphtheria. I'm off to send an ambulance to you. I've told Mary I will meet you at Olive Mount Hospital shortly.'

Harry closed the door behind the doctor and ran upstairs. Bella was packing a few bits in a bag and Mary was still holding on to Betty. 'Let's get her on the sofa in the sitting room, love,' Harry said, taking his tiny girl from Mary. 'Save them having to come up here.'

'Did he say what's wrong with her?' Mary asked; her face was white with worry.

'He's not sure, but we'll know soon enough,' Harry replied, not catching her eye.

'Well *I* know,' Mary said. 'I saw my little sister lose her life to it. And just listen to her trying to draw breath, Harry. She's gurgling; it's that hard for her.' She stopped as a clanging of bells sounded outside on the street.

'Ambulance is here,' Molly called up the stairs.

'Let the attendants in, love,' Harry called back. He dashed downstairs with Betty in his arms and handed her over to one of the two men; then they laid her on the stretcher they had brought in between them. They had a small tank of oxygen with them and they quickly popped a mask over Betty's face, tucked her in and carried the stretcher out to the waiting vehicle. Mary and Harry followed and climbed on board. Bella and Molly stood in the street, staring into the back of the ambulance, both crying.

'Just look after one another, we'll be back later,' Mary said to her worried girls as the attendant went to close the doors. 'Well your dad will, I'll stay with Betty as long as they'll let me.'

Bella put her arm around Molly's shoulders as they watched the ambulance speed away down the street 'Come on, Mol, let's go back inside.' She'd seen doors opening further down the street as neighbours came outside to see who was being taken into hospital. Bella didn't feel in the mood for talking to anyone right now. A feeling of dread for Betty settled in her stomach as she led Molly into the silent house and locked the front door.

Chapter Seven

Betty was rushed into theatre, where a surgeon performed a tracheostomy operation on her. A tube was inserted into the hole made in her windpipe at the front of her neck to allow oxygen to get into her lungs. Mary and Harry were allowed to wait in a small room off a nearby corridor until the operation was completed. On admission diphtheria had been diagnosed immediately and Betty admitted to isolation. Mary knew she wouldn't be allowed in to see her daughter, but had insisted that they wait until they heard further news. One of her friends from the domestic team came to the room to see them. Ethel Hardy was on a late shift.

'It's so good to see a familiar face, Ethel,' Mary greeted her pal, who had brought a tray through to them and sat down. Ethel poured three mugs of tea with extra sugar for shock and handed them round.

'I'm so sorry to hear about Betty, chuck,' Ethel said. 'What a worry for you both.'

Mary nodded. 'She couldn't breathe, poor little mite, she was making choking noises. It frightened the life out of me.' She took a sip of tea and Harry did the same.

'Well she's in the best place,' Ethel said. 'And at least with working here you can look at her through the windows when she goes into the isolation suite. It's more than most parents get to do.'

Harry nodded. 'Aye, she's right, Mary, it's better than nowt.'

Ethel finished her tea and got to her feet. 'I'd best get back and finish me cleaning. Good luck; and I'll see you soon.'

'Yes, thank you, Ethel. And thanks for the tea. It's much appreciated.'

'They're taking a long time in that theatre,' Harry said as Ethel left the room. He looked at the clock on the wall.

Mary chewed her lip anxiously. 'I thought that too, but I didn't like to say—' she broke off as a serious-faced white-coated doctor came into the room and closed the door behind him.

'I'm so very sorry, Mr and Mrs Rogers, we did all we could,' he began as the colour drained from Harry's face and Mary let out a loud and pitiful scream. 'But I'm afraid we couldn't save your daughter. Although the procedure was a success, Betty died of heart failure. This was possibly due to an undetected heart condition, and that in itself will have made her too weak to fight off the diphtheria. Do you have other children at home?'

'We do,' Harry answered, taking his distraught wife into his arms. 'Two older girls.'

'And did they share a room with Betty? Diphtheria is very contagious and anything Betty was in contact with will need to be destroyed. Once again, I'm really sorry for your loss. We'll arrange for someone to take you home now.'

'Can't we see Betty?' Mary sobbed. 'To say goodbye, like.'

'Not right now,' the doctor replied. 'But we will make arrangements with you to see her very soon.'

'But I want to see her now,' Mary cried. 'My little girl. What will I do without her?'

Tears running down his cheeks, Harry held his wife tight. 'Maybe it's to do with the risk of catching it, chuck. We need to get back to the girls so we can stop them touching anything at home that our Bets was in contact with. We can't take any chances, love. Come on, let's get back. Thank you, Doctor.'

The young doctor nodded his head, his eyes bright with unshed tears. He wished them both well and led them to the reception area, where someone was waiting to take them back to Victory Street.

*

Out in the communal backyard Harry poured paraffin over the bedding Mary had stripped off the girls' bed a couple of nights ago when they'd come back from the hospital after Betty's death.

Everything feared to be contaminated had been pushed into the metal dustbin right away and Mary had disinfected the mattress, after she'd removed the layers of rubber sheets underneath that kept it clean. The sheets had been in use in case Betty had an accident and meant the mattress had stayed protected and wouldn't need to be burned.

They couldn't afford a new one, so it was perhaps as well. The whole room had been practically fumigated and the bedding that wasn't being burned was in the kitchen steeping in strong bleach and boiling water in the tin bath that usually hung on the wall outside the back door. It was usually only brought inside once a week, on a Sunday night, for bath time in front of the back sitting room fire.

Keeping so busy was helping Mary to cope with her loss. Molly had stayed off school at the doctor's recommendation to make sure she wasn't incubating the disease, and Bella had stayed off work as a precaution too. Harry had taken a few days off as well, until after the funeral, so the whole family could be together to support each other.

Mary was walking around in a daze and Harry didn't know how she would ever come to terms with her loss. Betty had been a surprise baby but a very much loved one and they'd all doted on her. The house felt empty without their funny little one.

He choked on tears as he threw a lit match into the bin. The bedding caught fire immediately and he rammed the lid on. Smoke billowed out of the holes punched in the top. Mary had refused to part with Betty's much-loved teddy bear even though they'd been told to burn all toys that may have respiratory droplets on them. Instead the bear was soaking in a bucket of bleach and cold water by the back door. He was almost white now, like a polar bear, instead of the golden brown he'd once been.

Harry was worried about the cost of the funeral. They'd had no penny policy plan for a funeral on Betty like they had for Molly and Bella. When Betty arrived they'd struggled to feed another mouth and anything extra had to wait. Mary hadn't long been back at work once Betty started school and they just hadn't got around to getting a policy in place for her.

And besides, there wasn't really a rush because who would ever expect their five-year-old to go first, he thought. They would need to talk about it today, because the bill wouldn't go away, even though the undertaker who called yesterday to take the funeral details had told them not to worry. But he'd want paying at some point and Harry couldn't help *but* worry. Funerals were not cheap and although he hated thinking about Betty in those sorts of terms, it had to be done. He didn't want his little one lying in an anonymous pauper's grave.

*

'Our Bella, can you come and help me turn this mattress over, please,' Mary called down the stairs. She swiped a hand across her sweaty brow and took a deep breath. Bella joined her in the room and between them they tugged the mattress until it fell into place.

'Bet you'll be glad to sleep in your own bed tonight, chuck,' Mary said. Both girls had been sleeping on borrowed camp beds downstairs until Mary was certain the room was as clean as it could possibly be.

'I will, Mam,' Bella replied. 'But I won't half miss our little Bets snuggled in between us.' Bella's eyes filled and she wiped away her tears. 'I miss her all the time.'

'We all do, chuck. I don't know how I'm ever going to get over this. My little baby, gone, just like that. I wish I knew where she'd picked it up from but no one else in the school has been diagnosed or anyone local that we know of. It's very worrying because someone must be a carrier, but who? I was concerned that I'd brought it home from the hospital but they've said I didn't. Any patients in isolation in there haven't been anywhere near me and I haven't handled anything they've been in contact with.'

Bella shook her head. 'Mam, you'll make yourself ill if you keep worrying about it. It's just one of those things and I don't suppose we'll ever know.'

'I'm sure you're right, love. But one thing I do know now. I'm not sending our Molly away when they start evacuating. I want my girls here with me. I'm not losing anybody else.'

'Molly will be glad about that, Mam. She said last night she didn't want to go. She was all upset about it and wants to stay here with us.'

'Bless her, does she? Well that's settled then. The vicar is coming later to talk to us. Will you go down to the bakery for me, love, and get a nice cake to cut up? He'll like that.'

'Of course, Mam.'

'Thanks queen. You've been such a help. I want to ask you a favour as well before he comes. Our Betty loved it when you sang to her at bedtime. So will you sing her favourite song at the funeral for her?'

Bella swallowed hard. 'You mean "Over the Rainbow". Oh, God, Mam. It makes me cry at the best of times, but I'll do my best, I promise.'

*

As the vicar was preparing to leave that evening Bella answered a knock at the door. Bobby, clutching a large bunch of flowers, and his mother Fenella Harrison, who looked a little unsure of herself and her welcome, were standing there. Well at least the house was all ready for visitors.

Mam had worked her socks off and a fire had been lit in the best front parlour, so Bella smiled and greeted them, happy to see Bobby's concerned face. She'd missed him.

'Hello, come on in. Mam and Dad are just speaking with the vicar, so follow me, and then I'll take you into the parlour.' She led them into the back sitting room, where Molly was reading a book, stretched out on the sofa. 'Move, Molly. Let the visitors sit down. Go and put the kettle on for more tea.'

Molly jumped up and put her book on the table, smiling at Bobby and his mother, who sat down.

'My favourite book when I was Molly's age.' Mrs Harrison pointed to Molly's copy of *Little Women*. 'My mother bought me that for my ninth birthday and I devoured it. I treasured that book until one day two of my horrible older brothers snatched it from me and made paper aeroplanes with some of the pages. I don't think I ever really got over it,' she finished quietly.

Bobby raised an eyebrow in Bella's direction and gave a slight shrug of his shoulders. 'You never mentioned any of that before, Mum.'

Mrs Harrison looked embarrassed. 'Oh, it was just seeing the book again, it evoked a memory from long ago. That's all.' She dismissed the subject and fell quiet as goodbyes were heard coming from the hallway and the sound of the front door closing.

Bella opened the sitting room door and beckoned her parents into the room. 'Mam, we've got visitors,' she announced. 'Molly's just making a fresh pot of tea.'

Mrs Harrison got to her feet and held out her hand, which Mam took and shook gently. 'My dear Mrs Rogers, Bobby has some flowers for you all. From the ladies of the WI, along with our most sincere condolences.'

'Oh, er, well thank you very much,' Mam said, her eyes filling. 'That's very kind of you. Will you thank the others for me? Please come into the parlour. There's a nice fire in there and it's more comfortable than in here. That sofa's seen better days with the springs coming through.' The visitors were clearly making Mam anxious as she was talking ten to the dozen. She led the way and gestured to her decent suite of furniture that was only used for special occasions like Christmas. 'Please take a seat. Bella, you go and help Molly with the tea and slice the rest of that Victoria sponge cake up.'

Bella hurried to help Molly. Fancy Bobby and his mother turning up like that out of the blue! It was nice of them to bring flowers as well. Molly set the tray nicely with matching cups and saucers and Bella rooted out some side plates for the cake, which she finished slicing on the big plate it stood on. 'You carry the cake and plates and I'll do the tray. It's a bit heavy. When you've put the cake down bring the dirty pots through from the vicar's visit, okay?'

Molly nodded and made her way to the front parlour. She pushed open the door with her hip. Bobby jumped up to assist her and took the plates and cake. Molly picked up the used stuff as instructed by Bella and dashed back out of the room to the sanctuary of the old sofa and her book.

'Aren't you joining us?' Bella asked as she carried the tray through the back room.

Molly shook her head. 'Mam will start crying again and I can't stand it. Makes me cry too and then she gets even worse. You can do it for both of us. See what they want.'

'Okay, love.' Bella went back in and set the tray down on the small coffee table and proceeded to pour the tea, catching Bobby's eye as she looked up to enquire how many sugars they took.

'None for Mother, two for me,' he replied. 'Your mum just said you are going to sing at Betty's funeral.'

Bella nodded and chewed her lip. 'I'm going to try and do my best,' she said quietly.

'Well in that case, would you like me to sing with you? The choir will be at the service, so we two can sing "Over the Rainbow" for Molly. I'd like to, if it might make it easier for you.'

Bella smiled. 'Would you really do that? Oh, it would be lovely and I'd feel so much better. Thank you.'

'It'll be my pleasure,' Bobby said. 'She loved it when we sang it here for your birthday.'

'Now, please don't be offended by what I'm about to suggest,' Mrs Harrison said and took a sip of tea as Mam and Dad glanced enquiringly at her. 'The ladies of Wavertree WI would like to know if they can provide you with a small wake after the funeral in the church hall. They will supply a rather splendid buffet. We have some excellent cake and pastry-makers among our members who have offered their services free of charge.'

Mam's mouth fell open and she clutched Dad's hand. 'We're not in the least offended, are we Harry?' she said, speaking for them both. 'In fact, that's a huge weight lifted from our shoulders. Thank you, so much.'

'You have no idea how much this means to us,' Dad said, emotion catching his voice. 'This, er, unexpected tragedy happening to us is something we were totally unprepared for.'

'Indeed. I doubt anyone is prepared for the sad loss of so young a child,' Mrs Harrison said. 'I can't imagine how you are coping.'

Mam nodded. 'People say it will hit us harder at the funeral. We've been so busy since the day she, well she passed away, and they say keeping busy helps, but that it's after when it catches you.'

'Well if there's anything we can do to help, please don't hesitate to get in touch. We'll leave you in peace for now; we don't want to intrude any further. I'll be in contact for numbers of mourners, or Bobby will, and then I can let the ladies of the WI know for their catering purposes.' She got to her feet and Mam got up and gave her a hug.

'Thank you for your concern and support,' Mam said. 'I'll see you soon.'

Bella showed them out and Bobby squeezed her hand and whispered that he'd see her in a day or two.

'Bobby must bring you to tea, Bella, when things get a little more settled for you here,' Mrs Harrison said and gave a little wave as she walked away. Bobby smiled and hurried after her. Bella stared up the street as they got into a car parked several doors down and she realised that Bobby's dad was sitting in the driving seat.

She wondered why he hadn't come in, but maybe he'd dropped them off and been somewhere else meantime before coming back to pick them up. She watched the car move away and turn the corner at the bottom. Back inside she cleared the pots from the front parlour and took them into the kitchen to wash, her mind buzzing with the fact Bobby was going to help her sing Betty's favourite song. It felt comforting to know that.

*

'Well I wasn't expecting all that,' Mary said, shaking the cushions on the parlour sofa. 'But how nice of the WI ladies to offer to help us out with the wake. She's turned out quite nice, has Elsie Carter, in spite of her upbringing.'

Harry nodded and lit a cigarette. 'Funny how she never batted an eyelid though, you know, let on that she knew you from years ago. But still, maybe she doesn't like to think about her Old Swan days. She's done a grand job bringing up her lad. He's smashing is young Bobby. And he seems quite sweet on our Bella. Nice that they're going to sing for our little 'un as well.'

'It is. It'll help her because I know she'll struggle. But with regards to Elsie – or I should say, Fenella – I'm very grateful to her for her kindness today.'

Chapter Eight

After the beautiful service, attended by her family, neighbours and some of her young classmates, Betty was laid to rest in the same grave as her paternal grandparents in St Mary's churchyard. Bella stood beside Bobby, who had helped her get through the emotional ordeal of singing her sister's favourite song, while the vicar said a prayer. Her parents led the way into the church hall, asking the mourners to follow them. Bobby's mother was waiting with two other members of the WI to welcome everyone inside.

The buffet was laid out on two trestle tables and was plentiful. When word had been passed around the close-knit community that the WI were providing the wake for Betty, many neighbours had made contributions to help as well as collecting door to door and providing beautiful floral tributes that would be laid on top of the grave. Bella could see that her parents were overwhelmed by the kindness being shown to them on the saddest day of their lives.

People stopped her and Bobby as they walked into the hall, and praised their singing. Her mam's workmate Ethel Hardy put her arms around Bella and hugged her.

'There's not much makes me cry, gel, but you and him sang like angels back there. It was beautiful. Thank you.'

Bella smiled and Bobby shook Ethel's hand. 'It wasn't easy,' Bella said, 'but we got there.'

As Bobby turned to talk to someone else who had tapped his arm, Ethel whispered to Bella, 'He's sweet on you, gel and he's a good one. Don't let him go.'

Bella felt her cheeks heating as Ethel moved away to talk to one of their neighbours. People did seem to think she and Bobby were courting. *She* didn't mind, but would *he*? He'd not even kissed her yet, apart from a peck on the cheek. She went to stand by her mam and dad, who were with Molly near the buffet table.

'Would you like something to eat and a cuppa, love?' her dad asked. 'This all looks very nice, doesn't it? There's enough food to feed an army. They're spoiling us.'

'I'll have a cuppa, Dad. I'll get something to eat later on. I just feel a bit sort of churned up inside at the moment.'

'That's understandable, chuck.' He handed her a cup and saucer. 'Milk and sugar are over there.' He pointed to the end of the table, where Bobby's mother was standing talking to another WI lady. 'Just help yourself.'

Mrs Harrison turned and smiled at Bella as she approached. 'Well done, dear. You did your sister proud. The singing was beautiful.'

'Oh, thank you. Bobby did most of it. I struggled.'

'The emotion in your voice made the song very meaningful. Me, and the rest of my ladies here, were standing at the back of the church sharing that special moment.'

Bella blinked away a tear. She felt too choked to speak. But Mrs Harrison seemed to understand and handed her a clean white handkerchief from her pocket. She patted Bella's arm and picked up the teapot to refill it.

Two weeks before Christmas Molly celebrated her thirteenth birthday on the Saturday and as a treat, Bella took her to the Abbey picture house to see *The Wizard of Oz*. The newsreel shown before the film started was all about the conflict in Europe, which looked awful, and which Britain was now calling the Phoney War.

Nothing much seemed to be happening here apart from the underlying threat. There were regular air raid drills, all the windows of local houses and shops were covered in criss-cross tape and Mam had sewn blackout linings to all the curtains in the house. Any planes flying overhead were viewed with suspicion, but were usually test runs for the new Halifax Bombers being built nearby.

Bella and her friends were still singing regularly at work to keep morale up and it was getting harder to find new songs. The same ones were suggested over and over again. One man had brought his squeezebox in and another had a mouth organ, so they at least had a bit of a band on the go at break times. Everyone said how good the threesome was getting and they should try to do a few nights' work in the social clubs around Liverpool.

Dad had put his foot down when Bella had brought up the subject at home. 'No daughter of mine is going singing in a licensed establishment until she's older,' he'd replied, refusing to discuss it further. And that had been the end of it, for now. Bella turned her attention to something Molly was saying. The newsreel had finished and an usherette was making her way to the front of the circle where the girls were seated.

'Mam said we could have an ice-cream tub, remember,' Molly said.

Bella rooted in her purse for the shilling Mam had given her for the ice creams. 'Do you want to get them?' she suggested.

Molly nodded gleefully and joined the queue that was forming down the aisle. The lights had gone up slightly and Bella took a look around to see if there was anyone she recognised. But the picture house was half empty. That was unusual for a Saturday matinee, but times were hard and money tight. People were hanging on to what bit they'd got, just in case.

Molly was soon back with the tubs of ice cream and they settled down to watch the film. Bella didn't even bother to try to stop the tears that ran freely down her cheeks as Judy Garland sang 'Over the Rainbow'. She'd tried to be strong for everyone else over the last few weeks, blocking her own grief, but today it just overwhelmed her.

She looked at Molly, who was also sobbing quietly, and, reaching for her hand, she gave it a squeeze. Molly squeezed back. 'We've still got each other,' she whispered. Bella nodded.

Later, as they left the Abbey and strolled silently down the street, Molly sighed. 'Do you think our Betty is flying high with the bluebirds now, in that lovely place over the rainbow?'

'I'm sure she is, Mol. That's how we'll think of her, flying high with the bluebirds, and it will make us smile and remember her funny little ways.'

The head foreman, George Barratt, beckoned Bella across the factory floor and into a small office. He closed the door and offered her a seat. 'Don't look so worried,' he began. 'You're not in any bother. We're having the usual Christmas party in the canteen next week. But we thought instead of just doing a bit of dancing to the gramophone it might be nice if you three girls could give us a turn. Harry will do a bit on his squeezebox and Bert can tell a few jokes. Now what about asking that boyfriend of yours if he'll come and do a song or two with you? I've heard people say how good you are together.'

Bella chewed her lip. 'Well he's not actually my boyfriend, we're just good pals, but I'll ask Bobby if he'd like to come.'

'That'll be smashing. My mate's got an old piano his missus wants to get rid of and he said we could have it and keep it here. He's also got a horse and cart that he does his rag and bone round with, so him and his lad are going to fasten it to that and bring it over here and then we can see if it needs a bit of tuning and have it ready in time. We'll keep it here then, instead of him selling it on, and we can use it for singsongs at break times as well as the party. The workforce have all said how it keeps their spirits up and if things take a turn for the worse next year then we'll need it more than ever.'

'Oh that sounds great,' Bella said. 'I'll be seeing Bobby tomorrow night for our singing class and I'll ask him then.'

'Smashing. Now off you go and get some work done and have a think about what you can sing. Have a word with the other girls at break. Perhaps a few Christmas carols would be nice as well.'

'What can we wear?' Fran said as the three friends sat in the canteen. Bella had broken the news about the party and them performing for the rest of the workforce and that she'd been asked to invite Bobby along as well. She'd been worried that Fran would pull a face at that, but both she and Edie had eagerly agreed to the plan. 'We should all try and wear similar clothes, matching colours at least. What have we all got that's red? It's a nice Christmassy colour.'

'Nothing at all,' Bella said with a sigh. 'I've got a nice deep blue silky dress that Mam made me from some material she was given at work. It's for singing at Christmas with the choir in the church hall. They're doing a bit of a show as well. There are some soldiers in the area and they've been invited to come along.'

'Not Germans I hope,' Fran said and shuddered.

'Of course not.' Bella laughed. 'I don't know where they're from but it's somewhere in England and they are billeted locally, that's all I know. Anyway, back to the dress situation.'

'I've got a kingfisher blue dress with a full skirt and a sweetheart neckline,' Edie said. 'I've only worn it once and it's really nice.'

Fran nodded. 'Well in that case I'll go and see if I can find myself a blue dress at Paddy's on Saturday morning and in the afternoon you can both come to my place and we'll try them on and see what we think. It'll do me for Christmas Day for Frankie's mam's party as well. I was going to buy a new dress for that occasion anyway so that's just perfect. I want to look nice for him because he's talking about definitely signing up next year, so it could be the only Christmas we get to spend together for quite some time.'

Edie picked up her mug of tea and took a sip. 'Oh Fran, I hope this won't be your last Christmas together. Quite a few of the lads from the factory floor have said they're signing up too as soon as Christmas is out of the way. There's only going to be women left at this rate to run this factory.'

Fran sighed. 'My two older brothers have mentioned it but Mam clipped them both around the ears and said she was putting her foot down and they can't go. She needs the money they earn at the docks, she said. But to be honest she can't really stop them.'

'Has your mam signed your Alfie up to the evacuation programme yet?' Bella asked Fran. 'Mam won't let Molly go; not now she's lost Betty. It would crack her up if anything happened to Molly too.'

'She might not have a choice,' Fran said. 'We'll have to see what happens. They've already sent a lot of kids to the country with the first evacuation and that was a waste of time because nothing much has happened here yet. Our neighbour's two young daughters have gone to Shropshire, wherever that is. Anyway,' she finished as the end-of-break bell rang out. 'That's us with our outfits planned. Now we just need to choose the songs and some for you and Bobby, if he'll come. We three can get some practice in at my place and work out the harmonies between us.'

'So what do you think?' Bella asked Bobby as they strolled up Grosvenor Road towards the church hall.

'I think it's a wonderful idea and I'll be happy to join you girls. Especially if I'm to sing a duet or two with *you*.'

'Really? Oh, Bobby, that's great. We'll give the workers a really good night. They deserve it. They all work so hard and there's not a lot to smile about right now, is there?'

'No, indeed. It's been a harrowing year all round. Especially for your own family, Bella.'

She nodded, feeling her eyes filling up. She blinked rapidly and half-smiled.

He stopped walking and looked at her. 'Now don't feel offended by this, but my mother said it won't be an easy time for you all this Christmas and being in a house where your little sister should be will be hard to cope with. She wants me to ask if you would all like to come to us on Christmas Day for dinner and a light supper later.'

Bella stared at him, wide-eyed. She still hadn't been to his house yet as time had flown and they had all been so busy. But the big houses on Prince Alfred Road always looked lovely around Christmas time, with twinkling candles on the trees that stood in the tall Georgian windows. She'd often wondered what it would be like to live in one of the houses. Spending Christmas Day in Bobby's home would be lovely. It would save Mam worrying about them affording enough to eat as well. She'd been counting the pennies the other day and shaking her head. She and Dad were still trying to pay off the debt of Betty's funeral and were struggling, even with the undertaker knocking the price down to half of what it would have normally cost.

'Bobby, that sounds lovely. I most certainly would love to say yes, but will you come home with me later and then you can give the invitation to them yourself?'

'Consider it done,' he said, smiling. 'Believe you me; you will be doing me a huge favour as well. They always fall asleep after dinner and that leaves me bored to tears for the rest of the day. They won't dare do that with visitors. I'll really look forward to it.'

Chapter Nine

December 1939

Mary was standing in the kitchen up to her elbows in pastry-making as Bella walked in from work. 'Hiya, chuck. Just thought I'd make something for you to take into work tomorrow to help with the food for the party. It won't be much, a few sausage rolls and some cheese straws. Better than nothing though, eh?'

'Oh, Mam, that's smashing, thank you.' Bella came over to hug her mother. 'Everyone is bringing a bit of food to put on the buffet table. It all helps. I didn't like to ask if I could take something in, well, with you watching the pennies for Christmas.'

'I know, love. But us going to Bobby's mam's will be a big weight off our shoulders, money-wise. We'll still take some mince pies and a bottle of sherry though. I don't want to show my face empty-handed. It's not polite. But at least we know we'll get a good dinner.'

'I'm so glad you said yes. I'm really looking forward to it,' said Bella.

'I still can't get over the fact she's asked us round. I mean, we haven't spoken since we were at school. I left the Old Swan area when I married your dad and came to live in Wavertree and she just seemed to vanish into thin air. Then next thing I hear, she's married to an air-force bloke, Wing Commander Harrison, no less, changed her name and moved into one of the posh houses opposite The Mystery.'

'You never saw her again?' Bella asked.

'No, I've no idea what happened to her or her family in between, but it's not my place to ask and unless she wants to tell me herself, I'm not going to be nosy. She hasn't even let on that she knows who I am yet, so it's best to let sleeping dogs lie unless *she* brings up the subject.'

Bella nodded her agreement and took off her scarf and coat. She hung them on the hall stand and went back into the kitchen. 'I'll have a bite to eat with everyone and then I'm going to Fran's with Edie to pin-curl our hair and put some nice varnish on our nails, so we're ready for tomorrow night. We won't have time before the party. I'll be staying at Bryant's and not coming home at teatime as there's no point. We'll get changed in a spare office and we'll be having the buffet, so at least I'll get something to eat. Bobby's dad will come and collect us later on and bring us all home.'

'That's very good of him,' Mary said. 'He seems a nice man. Bet Bobby takes after him.'

Bella smiled. 'I think maybe he does.'

'Has he not asked you out properly yet? To do a bit of courting, I mean?'

'Mam,' Bella said, blushing furiously. 'You know he hasn't or I would have asked you if it's okay. We're simply good friends, that's all. He's very caring and nice but I don't think he's looking for a proper girlfriend at the moment.'

'Hmm, is that right?' Mary muttered under her breath. 'We'll see.'

Bella linked Edie's arm as they hurried round to Fran's house. She was looking forward to a nice night, just the three of them. A good gossip and playing around with their hair and nails was just what they all needed to give them a morale boost.

'Are you looking forward to tomorrow night?' Edie asked.

'Sort of. I'm a bit nervous, but it should be fun. And at least we know the audience likes us. Well, we assume they do.' Bella laughed.

'Come on in, gels,' Fran's brother Donald said, flinging the door open at their knock. 'She's in the back room with Mam. Go through.'

'Thanks, Don,' Bella said and led the way into the warm and cosy back sitting room, where Grandma Jackson was dozing in her usual chair by the fire.

'Evening, girls, take a seat. There's a fresh brew in the pot and a few biscuits on that plate there.' Mrs Jackson pointed to the table that was set with tea things. 'We've got some pin-curl clips and my home-made sugar and water setting lotion at the ready and our Fran picked up a nice bottle of red nail varnish on Saturday when she got her new dress. I've turned the hem up and pulled the bodice darts in a bit and it fits her a treat now. I think you'll do them proud tomorrow. I hope someone manages to take a photo of you all dressed up. I wish we had a decent camera that takes photos indoors.'

'Perhaps the foreman will bring one in, Mam,' Fran said, pouring tea out for her friends. 'When we've had this will you pin Bella's hair up and I'll do Edie's and then you can do mine and then by the time we've done each other's nails our hair will be ready to comb out. The setting lotion will have dried off and we should have nice waves.'

Mrs Jackson nodded. 'I'll get Grandma to bed while you finish your tea. Come on, Gran.' She woke her gently, helped her to her feet and led her out of the room. The front parlour here was converted to a bedroom for Grandma.

The house was overcrowded with the two older boys, young Alfie, and Fran as well. It was slightly bigger than Bella's home in that there was a small third bedroom that Fran slept in. At least all her brothers had gone upstairs out of the way and there was no sign of her dad, so they had the back room to themselves for now.

Bella reached for a ginger biscuit and dunked it in her tea. 'Mam's baked some things to take in for the buffet tomorrow,' she announced.

'That's nice of her,' Edie said. 'I've got some crackers and cheese to take in and Fran's mam said she's making some sarnies first thing in the morning so that they'll be fresh. The cook can put them in her fridge in the canteen then. Should be a good spread if we all take stuff in.'

'I'm really looking forward to it,' Fran said, smiling. 'Wish I could ask Frankie to come but it's for staff only; well, apart from your Bobby.' She raised an eyebrow in Bella's direction.

'He's *not* my Bobby,' Bella said. 'We're just good friends. I keep telling everyone that but no one takes any notice,'

'So he hasn't asked you out yet?' Fran said. 'Taking his bloody time, isn't he?'

Bella sighed. 'No, he hasn't. We go to the pictures now and again and our singing classes of course, but nothing else.'

'And would you like to go out with him properly?' Edie asked. 'I'd have thought by now the pair of you would be doing a bit of courting.'

'Yes, well we're not. And I'm not sure why, but that's the way it is, so don't keep going on about it.' Bella folded her arms, dismissing the subject. She didn't understand why Bobby hadn't suggested they have a proper date either, but nothing had been said and it wasn't up to her to ask him. Nice girls just didn't do that sort of thing.

'You don't know what you're missing,' Fran said, lowering her voice, a dreamy look in her eyes. 'Me and Frankie can't keep our hands off one another. We haven't, well, you know, done anything yet. But if he has to go away when he joins up, then I think we will do, before he leaves.'

Edie stared at her wide-eyed. 'You just be careful. You don't want to be taking any chances. Your mam would go mad if you got yourself in the family way and he's nowhere to be seen.'

Fran rolled her eyes. 'He's not that stupid, Edie, and neither am I.'

'Even so—' Edie stopped as Mrs Jackson came back into the room.

'That's her settled for the night,' Mrs Jackson said. 'Right, let's clear this table and get on with the hair-styling, shall we?' She cleared the pots away and Fran sorted out the pin-curl clips, and draped a towel each around Edie and Bella's shoulders.

Mrs Jackson came back into the sitting room with a tail comb and gave the bowl of sugar and water a stir. 'Right, Bella, let's get you sorted.' She dipped the comb in the water and pulled it through the ends of Bella's hair. Then, while Fran did Edie's, Mrs Jackson deftly wound loops of hair around her fingers and pinned the curls up with the clips all around Bella's head. 'There, that won't take long to dry. It's nice and warm in here so we'll leave them clips in until we're ready to comb you out. Go and sit on the rug in front of the fire and keep turning your head around while the heat gets to it all over. We'll put a hairnet on you for going home and to keep on overnight. Have you brought a headscarf for walking home?'

Bella nodded. Fran finished Edie's hair and then sat down while her mam pinned hers up. Edie joined Bella on the rug. By the time Fran was ready they had bright red cheeks and were both sweating cobs.

'Come and sit at the table, girls, while our Fran dries her hair, and we'll make a start on your nails,' Mrs Jackson said. 'I'll give them a bit of a file with an emery board and then our Fran will do the rest.'

'Thanks for having us over, Mrs Jackson, it's really kind of you,' said Bella.

'It's a pleasure, girls.' She smiled and then yawned. 'I'm going to get off to bed shortly. I'm really tired. Your dad will be back from the pub any minute, Fran. It's his darts team meeting tonight and he's never usually too late home because he needs to be up early for work.'

She set to with the emery board and Bella and Edie's nails were soon nicely shaped and ready for the first coat of nail varnish. 'I'll do yours while you're still on the floor,' she said and knelt down besides Fran and filed her nails too. 'Right, you're all done now. Just be careful putting the varnish on, take your time and let it dry fully in between coats and it'll look lovely.'

She got to her feet, groaning as her knees creaked when she righted herself. 'Flipping rheumatics, mind you, kneeling on the floor doesn't help. You girls make the most of being young because when you get to my age it all starts to go downhill.'

Fran laughed. 'Mam, you're not at all bad for forty-one. You can give a lot of 'em younger than you a run for their money.'

As Bella, Fran and Edie got ready in the small office space they'd been allocated just off the canteen their excitement mounted, mixed with a feeling of nervousness. They zipped up each other's dresses, smoothed down full skirts, made sure the seams were straight on their stockings and fluffed out their curls, which had been protected by loosely fastened turbans all day. There was no full-length mirror available, so they took it in turns to stand on a chair and gaze into a mirror fastened to the wall. They slicked on lipstick that matched the red of their nails and rubbed a touch into their cheeks to add a blush.

'Do you think we look okay?' Fran asked as Bella opened the door and pulled Bobby, who was waiting outside and making sure no one walked in on them, inside.

He nodded and whistled. 'You all look amazing. Like true professionals.'

'Thank you,' Bella said with a laugh. 'I know our dresses aren't the same blue, but I think we blend well together and the styles are similar.'

Bobby gave them an appraising look. 'Well you kind of go down the scale of blues, dark, medium and light,' he said, 'and you match my navy suit. So that was good fortune that I chose this one.'

Fran laughed. 'It blooming well was. Right,' she said as clapping sounded from the makeshift theatre in the canteen, 'that's Harry finished with his squeezebox turn. Are we ready, ladies?'

A knock at the door had them all jumping to attention and Bobby opened it.' The foreman, George Barratt, stood there, mopping his forehead with a hanky.

'Didn't like to just barge in with the ladies getting changed in here,' he announced. 'But we're about ready if they are. I'll introduce the gels first, Bobby; they can do their spot, then we'll have the buffet and after that I'll bring you and Bella on together for your duets. Then you can all finish the night together with a finale.'

He straightened his bow tie, clicked the heels of his shiny black shoes together, did a little bow and walked back to the area designated for the stage, where he was compèring the show. He walked to the microphone that he'd borrowed from his mate who managed the Speke British Legion club, cleared his throat and one-two-ed as someone shouted good-naturedly, 'Gerron with it!'

He smiled. 'Now I know you all like the Boswell Sisters and the Andrews Sisters, but tonight, to entertain you for the first time in Liverpool, we are bringing to you the one and only – the Bryant Sisters.' A cheer went up, followed by loud wolf whistles and clapping as the girls ran forward to join him.

Bella smiled. They hadn't even thought to choose a name and she nodded enthusiastically at George's well-thought-out choice. They were in Bryant & May's, after all.

'Thanks, George,' Bella whispered. 'That name is perfect. What else could we be?' She spoke into the microphone. 'Good evening, everybody. Oh come on, you can do better than that,' she said as a ripple of voices greeted her. 'GOOD EVENING!'

More clapping and whistling and Bella nodded to the pianist, who they'd rehearsed with over several lunchtimes since the piano had arrived. He knew the key they preferred to sing in and struck up with 'Alexander's Ragtime Band.' The audience joined in and a few got up to dance.

Following the cheering and applause that followed, Fran and Edie grinned at each other as Bella spoke to the audience and then announced the next song. She was a natural leader and they let her do the talking in between the songs. By the time they finished their spot with 'He's Got the Whole World in His Hands' everyone was on their feet waving their arms and singing along.

George's grin was splitting his face as he walked over to them. They bowed and smiled and waved as the audience called for more.

As soon as they came off, Bobby gave them a group hug as they all talked at once. George announced the buffet was ready; to queue patiently as there was plenty for everybody, and that the show would continue in half an hour.

'Shall we get something to eat?' Fran said, pointing to the buffet tables set out against the back wall of the canteen. 'Me stomach thinks me throat's been cut.'

Bella shook her head. 'I can't eat until after we've done our next spot. I get too nervous to eat anything. It might make me sick.'

Bobby nodded. 'Me too. I'll wait until later. That was fabulous, girls. They all enjoyed your performance.

'I really enjoyed doing it,' Edie said. 'Beats packing matches any day. It would be smashing to earn a living doing something we love like this instead of having no choice because my mam needs the money.'

Bella sighed. 'Wouldn't it just. Ah well, it's nice to perform properly tonight instead of on the factory floor.'

When Bobby and Bella took their places in front of the microphone the room fell silent. George had announced them as the new Bing Crosby and Connee Boswell. They began with the popular duo's 'An Apple for the Teacher', immediately followed by 'Swinging on a Star'. The applause was tumultuous and Bella felt the lump in her throat threatening to choke her. She couldn't believe how much the audience were enjoying this. They sang 'Paper Doll' next and finished with Bob Hope and Shirley Ross's 'Thanks for the Memory'. Couples got up to waltz, singing along. Bobby gave Bella a squeeze at the deafening applause and shouts of 'More!' 'Shall we?' he whispered. 'Can you manage it?'

She nodded and took a deep breath. 'I think so. Let's do it for Betty.'

He smiled. 'Thank you so much,' he addressed the audience. 'We'd like to sing one more song for you now and we dedicate this to the memory of Bella's little sister, Betty. It was her favourite song.' He nodded at the pianist; a gentle ripple of applause went around the room and silence fell as everyone listened to 'Over the Rainbow'. At the end, when everyone got to their feet and cheered, Bella blinked rapidly as Bobby squeezed her hand and whispered, 'Well done.'

George thanked the pair and announced that while they took a short break before the finale he was going to do the raffle.

Bella dashed off to the ladies' cloakroom while Bobby got them some food from what was left. He took the plate over to a table in the corner, where Fran and Edie were sitting with a middle-aged man in a suit who was smoking a cigar. Bobby had seen the man earlier when he was talking to George. He smiled and said hello.

'Good evening, young man,' the man said. 'I'm Chas Morris, George's mate who lent him the microphone.'

Bobby smiled politely and took a bite of sausage roll, savouring the flaky pastry. 'I didn't realise how hungry I was,' he said as Bella joined them and picked up a sandwich.

She took a peep inside it. 'Spam and tomato, yum. I'm feeling hungry now.' She wolfed it down and took a swig of lemonade that Fran had poured her from the jug on the table. 'Oh, that's better,' she said with a sigh.

'This is Chas, he's George's friend,' Bobby said, introducing them.

'I'm honoured to be here tonight as it's workers only, apart from Bobby, I believe,' Chas said. 'However, there's a reason for it. I run the British Legion club in Speke and I'm always looking for good acts to put on when I do a special Saturday night show. George suggested I come and see you perform and give my opinion.'

All eyes turned to Chas as he continued. 'I've got to say that both your performances were the best I've seen in a long time. Most professional, in fact. Now I know that none of you are very old and certainly not of drinking age yet, but I'd like to invite you all to put on a show for me early next year, maybe on the first Saturday after New Year. I can come and speak with your parents if they have any objections and reassure them that I'll look after you. The money is good. I think you'd go down very well with my members.'

'Oh my God,' Fran said. 'I can't believe it. Really?'

'Yes, really,' Chas replied. 'It won't interfere with your daytime jobs as it's weekends only and if it takes off maybe you could do it once a month for me.'

'We'd need to discuss it with each other and then with our parents,' Bobby said. 'But I can't see why it would be a problem at all.'

Bella and Edie smiled gleefully. Bella recalled her dad's comments about his daughter not working on licensed premises, but maybe she could persuade him to change his mind. After all, the four of them would be together at all times and quite safe.

Chapter Ten

Christmas Day 1939

Mary frowned as Molly waltzed into the kitchen, flicking her hair back over her shoulders. 'Have you got lipstick on, miss?'

Molly blushed. 'Just a bit. Our Bella said it was all right.'

'Oh she did, did she? Well it's not all right. You're thirteen. I'm not having the Harrisons thinking I'm bringing up a tart. Wash it off right now.' She handed Molly a flannel from the draining board. 'And then rinse that flannel out when you've finished.'

Molly tutted but did as she was told. 'Just thought it looked nice, that's all. Seeing as we're going somewhere posh for our dinner.'

'Yes, well, you need to look smart, never mind posh.' Looking at her daughter, Mary softened. 'That dress is nice on you. Fits you better than it ever fitted our Bella, anyway.'

Molly nodded and looked down at the bottle-green fine wool dress she was wearing. It had been Bella's best dress for ages until she grew out of it. It was still in a nice condition because it had only ever been worn for special occasions and church on a Sunday, and Mary had stitched a Peter Pan collar in white to the neckline, which had given it a more modern look.

'Have you got a green ribbon for your hair up in that mess of a bedroom?' Mary asked.

'Aw, Mam, I don't want a ribbon in my hair. That's too babyish at my age.'

'Well, go and sit in the front parlour with your dad while I finish off in here and then we'll open the presents before we walk round to the Harrisons' for half past twelve.'

Mary sighed as she finished wiping round the sink and tipped the washing-up water away. She thought about her little Betty and how she'd have loved to have her hair tied up in ribbon bows today. It had been hard last night wrapping the presents and there being nothing under the tree in the parlour for her.

They'd got some flowers and greenery to take to the churchyard on the way out, to put on the grave. Her eyes filled and she swiped her hand across her face and filled the kettle. A quick cuppa before the present-opening would be nice and might make her feel better. She'd wrapped the mince pies she'd made to take with them in greaseproof paper, and a bottle of sherry that Harry had bought from the off-licence last night was wrapped in tissue paper, ready to go. Bella would be back from Fran and Edie's shortly. She'd just popped out to wish them a happy Christmas.

*

Fran's little brother Alfie let Bella in and then went back to playing with his Christmas presents on the sitting room floor. He was surrounded by lead soldiers and a wooden fort. The smell of seasonal cooking filled the air and Granny Jackson was sitting in her usual fireside chair, examining the dentures clasped in her hand. Bella's stomach lurched. She hated dentures. Her dad had a bottom set, to replace the teeth he'd lost and broken when he'd got into a fight in the school playground as a teenager, and they were dropped into a jam jar on the kitchen windowsill to soak each night, staring at her as she got washed or had a soak in the tin bath.

Mrs Jackson popped her head around the kitchen door.

'Morning, Bella. How's your mam today? Not going to be easy for her, it being the first Christmas without young Betty and all. Granny, put your bloody teeth back in!' She shook her head. 'Honestly, what to do with her at times, I do not know.'

Fran half-smiled. Missing Betty was one of the reasons she'd come out as the sadness was overwhelming at times like this. 'Mam's bearing up, thank you. We all are; the best we can. I'm glad we're going out for our dinner, at least it's a nice change for Mam and it will stop her getting too upset as the day goes on.'

'Best all round if you ask me. And you get to have a nosy in Fenella Harrison's house. Lucky you. Fran's in her bedroom. Go on up, love. It's a bit more peaceful than down here with our Alfie pretending he's a battalion fighting the Germans and what have you.'

Bella ran lightly up the stairs and knocked on Fran's door.

'Come in,' Fran called. Bella squeezed into the tiny back bedroom, where the bed was crammed under the window and jammed in by a chest of drawers at the end and a bedside table at the top. How on earth Mrs Jackson managed to change the bedding was anyone's guess, but she obviously did; the room was spotlessly clean and smelled fresh, like Fran herself always did.

'Morning, Merry Christmas,' Fran greeted her. 'Park yourself.' She was sitting on the bed touching up her nails with the same red varnish they'd worn for the show the other night. 'Got a few chips,' she said and moved over to make room for Bella. 'So, are you all ready for the royal dinner party?' she asked, waving her hands in the air to dry her nails.

'Oh, stop it,' Bella said with a giggle. 'I'm nervous enough as it is and Mam is acting like we really are going to royalty. Bet she'll hardly be able to stop herself curtseying.'

They both laughed and Fran picked up a box to show Bella the pretty silver charm bracelet that Frankie had given her for Christmas last night.

'Oh, that's so lovely. How thoughtful of him. Did he like *his* pressie?' Fran had shown her and Edie the gift she'd bought last week for Frankie. A silver St Christopher medallion on a chain, just in case he was sent abroad when he joined up, as he seemed determined to do. It would help to keep him safe, she hoped.

'He did. We got a bit weepy last night, well I did anyway. I had a large glass of sherry at his sister's and it went right to my head. Made me feel all over-emotional. Not used to it, you see. It was nice though, I have to admit. Maybe next time I'll eat something first.'

Bella smiled. 'Did you enjoy yourself at his sister's?'

'Yeah, she's really nice. Have you asked your mam and dad about us performing in the Legion yet? I thought I'd wait until after Christmas when it's a bit less fraught in this house and Mam won't be half as mithered.'

Bella nodded. 'That's what I'm doing too and I've just come from Edie's and she's kept it to herself for now as well. First week of January will be a good time. I suppose I'd better get back, I've been out over an hour. They'll be waiting to open their pressies before we go on the royal visit.'

Fran leaned over and gave Bella a hug. 'All the best. I hope everything goes well for you today. Can't wait to hear about it.'

Bella rolled her eyes. 'Can't say I'm looking forward to it really. It's a bit different to what we're used to. Must remember which knife and fork to use first, and all that. Be nice to see Bobby again though. I haven't seen him since we did the church hall show just after our works do. He's had family stuff on and we didn't go to church this morning as Mam was too upset. Anyway, I'll call in tomorrow with a news bulletin. Enjoy your day and have a good time tonight at Frankie's.'

Bella held Molly's hand while their mam and dad laid the flowers they'd brought on Betty's grave. Dad slipped his arm around Mam's waist and she leaned into him. Bella had never really thought about it before, but to lose a baby that you'd brought into the world, a baby that you'd loved with all your heart, must be the cruellest thing that could happen to any mother, and any father, come to that. Life could be so hard at times.

'Right then, are we ready?' Dad said, leading the way back down the short path to the church gates. 'Let's go and get it over then. I almost wish we were having our dinner at home now. I don't really feel like making small talk with people I don't know from Adam.'

'But you know Bobby, Dad, and you've met his mother,' Bella said. 'Come on, it'll be all right. And it saves Mam having to cook a dinner for us. It's a day off for her and she deserves that. Let's make the best of it.'

A tall woman in a black dress covered with a white apron opened the door to their ringing the bell at the rather grand Prince Alfred Road house as Bella peered in the window, admiring the heavily decorated Christmas tree that filled it. 'Please, do come in,' she said, smiling.

She took their coats and hung them in the small cloakroom that also housed a toilet and sink, but Mam kept hold of her shopping bag with the sherry and mince pies inside. 'Mrs Harrison is waiting in the drawing room. Follow me. Your guests, madam,' she announced, opening a door on the left at the end of a long hallway. Bella shook her head. There were more doors in this hall than they'd got in the whole of their Victory Street house. The woman stepped back to let them pass.

'Thank you, Margaret.' Mrs Harrison nodded towards the woman and invited the family to sit down. 'I'm afraid my husband had to pop out with Robert, but they will be back shortly. Now what can I get you to drink? Tea, coffee, or a drop of sherry perhaps?'

'Tea for me, please,' Mam said, reaching down for her brown paper carrier bag. 'And Harry'll have the same and so will the girls.

We don't want to put you to any trouble when you've got a dinner to get ready. Here, I've brought some sherry.' She pulled out the bottle and handed it over, missing the slightly raised eyebrow when Fenella looked at the label. 'Just as a thank-you,' Mam continued, 'and there's some mince pies I made in that bag as well.'

'Oh, well thank you, my dear. I'll take the bag through to the kitchen. Cook's preparing lunch in there, so she can put them in a tin. Back in a moment.'

'Now I feel a right fool,' Mam said, looking at her family. 'I presumed Mrs H would be doing the dinner, not a bloody cook. They've even got a waitress.'

'Aye,' Harry said, pulling at his collar and the tie he wasn't used to wearing. 'How the other half lives, eh?'

'Dad, shush,' Bella whispered as Molly giggled. She looked around the tastefully furnished room. A banked-up fire crackled and burned in the black-leaded grate that was set in a marble surround. Two large, light-coloured sofas sat either side, with a coffee table in the centre, placed on a red Persian rug.

A well-stocked bookcase took up one alcove near the chimney breast and a bureau filled the other. Framed pictures adorned the walls and lamps on small tables cast a glow in dark corners. The curtains at the windows were red velvet with gold tassels tying them back. *What a beautiful room*, Bella thought. Mrs Harrison had good taste.

'She's come a long way from that tatty little house in Old Swan with the torn bed sheets at the broken windows,' Mam muttered, shaking her head.

Mrs Harrison came back into the room. 'Margaret will bring the tea through shortly,' she said. 'Now, shall we have a nice bit of music on in the background? I believe the Light Programme has a carol service on at the moment. I'll tune the wireless in and then it can stay on for the king's speech after lunch.'

The door opened and Margaret pushed a polished wooden trolley on castors, laden with tea things, into the room.

Bella had never seen a trolley like that before. She spotted a small plate full of fresh shortbread fingers. Mrs Harrison poured the tea into delicate china cups decorated with pink roses. Bella could see the beads of sweat on her dad's face; probably terrified at the thought of holding such a delicate cup in his big hands, she thought. He was used to a chunky pint-sized mug with chips around the top from being dropped in the sink numerous times when Molly had done the washing up.

Mrs Harrison handed the cups and saucers out and Dad immediately placed his on the coffee table. 'Would anyone like a piece of shortbread? I understand it's only been out of the oven a short time and it smells delicious.'

Molly nodded and was handed a slice on a small china plate that matched the cups, along with a crisp white linen napkin. She thanked Mrs Harrison and tucked in, rolling her eyes in pleasure as she savoured the shortbread.

'What about you, Bella?' Mrs Harrison asked as Mam and Dad shook their heads and said 'no thank you' at the same time.

'Yes please, I would love some,' Bella said. 'It looks very nice.'

As they enjoyed their unexpected snack voices sounded in the hall, the door opened and Bobby popped his head into the room. 'Merry Christmas everyone.'

'Merry Christmas,' they chorused back.

'I'm so sorry I wasn't here to greet you. We had to make a mercy Father Christmas dash across Liverpool. My godfather and his daughter, who should have come to us last night for supper and to collect their presents, were taken ill and had to stay home. We couldn't let them be without something to unwrap on Christmas Day, so we delivered the gifts ourselves.'

'How are dear Howard and Alicia?' Mrs Harrison asked as Bobby sat down beside her on the sofa.

'Both a bit weary and Howard's cough is quite shocking. We've told him he needs to get the doctor in tomorrow if he's still as bad.

Alicia is picking up slightly but she's upset that she missed coming here last night.'

'Poor girl. Alicia's mother passed away two years ago and Howard also lost his mother recently,' Mrs Harrison told her guests. 'She was helping him to bring Alicia up, but now the two of them are alone. It's so tragic.'

'He needs to get some staff,' Bobby's father said, coming into the room. 'He's got the space to accommodate them. I told him not to be so bally tight and employ a cook and a maid so that Alicia isn't left to do it all on her own. It's not right.'

'How old is she?' Bella asked, imagining a young girl around Molly's age left to look after a big house, as it surely would be if it had the room for staff to live in.

'Alicia is the same age as Robert,' Mrs Harrison said. 'They've grown up together and were the best of friends as small children. Well, they *are* still very close, aren't you, darling?' She ruffled Bobby's hair as his cheeks turned pink. 'Our families always hoped that one day they'd be the perfect match. One never knows, does one?' She smiled at her husband, who smiled back.

Bella's stomach flipped as Margaret came back into the room. 'Madam, lunch is ready to serve,' she announced.

'Thank you, Margaret. We'll come through to the dining room. Follow me,' she instructed and walked away, leaving a waft of expensive perfume in her wake.

Bella and Bobby were last to leave the drawing room and she was conscious of him trying to catch her eye. He pulled on her arm to stop her walking into the hall.

'Err, what Mother said then,' he began, 'Just ignore her. She's living in cloud cuckoo land over Alicia and me and the future. It's never going to happen.'

Bella stared at him. Was Alicia the reason he'd never asked her out? It was the first she'd heard of her, so maybe it was all in his mother's head, but still. Mrs Harrison had seemed quite sure of herself and perhaps Bobby harboured feelings for Alicia that stopped him getting involved with Bella. Whatever the case was, she'd now lost her appetite, in spite of the wonderful aromas of food wafting down the hall from the open dining room doorway. 'You'd better go,' she told him. 'I'll just visit the cloakroom. See you in a minute or two.'

She dashed away into the small cloakroom that Margaret had hung their coats in and leaned her head on the tiled wall above the sink. She felt sick now, like someone had punched her in the stomach. She didn't want to join the others for dinner. Without giving it a second thought, she grabbed her coat and scarf and let herself out of the house, closing the door quietly behind her.

Outside, the cold air hit her. She ran across the nearby Mystery Park and didn't stop until she was home. Remembering her mam had the keys to the front door, she ran round the back into the yard and rooted under an old brick for the spare back door key. There was no one about; the neighbours were probably all inside tucking in to their Christmas dinners.

Bella let herself in and locked the door behind her. She ran upstairs and flung herself on the bed and burst into tears. Maybe she was overreacting, but the feeling of hurt when Bobby's mum had implied he was pretty much spoken for had knocked her for six. For months she'd been pretending to herself, and everyone else, that she didn't mind them being just friends. But now his mam had taken away all her dreams of a romantic future with him, as well as a singing career, that may have blossomed into something huge for them in time.

Chapter Eleven

Mary frowned at the empty chair where Bella should have been sitting. Where the devil *was* the girl? Bobby had come in and said she'd gone to the cloakroom, but that was ages ago. He'd looked a bit sheepish as he'd taken his place and he wasn't meeting anyone's eye. She wondered if they'd had words about that Alicia his mother had mentioned.

Mary knew her daughter was sweet on Bobby and her whole family and her friends thought he felt the same for Bella. Although he'd never asked her out. She'd thought that odd as they were always together, but just as good friends, she'd always said, and she'd put it down to him being maybe a bit shy. Now it seemed there was good reason why, and Bobby hadn't bothered to mention there was another girl in his life that he was close to.

'Excuse me.' She got to her feet. 'I'm just going to see where Bella is.' She left the room and went to knock on the cloakroom door. When she got no response Mary pushed the door open and peered inside. Bella's coat and the bright red scarf she'd been wearing earlier were gone from the peg.

Mary took a deep breath and wondered what to do. It would be rude to just walk out and besides, she was starving and that beautiful food on the table would go to waste. Bella would have gone home and she might want to be alone while she had either a good cry or a good think. She'd have to go back into the dining room and make up an excuse.

They could eat their dinner and get away straight after. That way they wouldn't need to sit around making small talk, which she knew was inevitable and she also knew was something Harry was dreading. They were like fish out of water here and no matter how kind the offer when it was issued, they should have said no and stayed in their own little home with the memories of Betty all around them. She'd have managed somehow to produce a decent dinner.

Back in the dining room Mary coughed to gain attention and, all eyes on her, she began to lie. 'I just found Bella in the cloakroom feeling rather unwell. I've packed her off home to go straight to bed. I'm really sorry about her dinner getting wasted but I felt it was for the best.'

Everyone showed their sympathy. 'We can ask Margaret to wrap a parcel of food for you to take home for Bella for later,' Mrs Harrison said. 'You can heat it up for her supper maybe.'

'Thank you, that's very kind of you,' Mary said, trying to catch Bobby's eye. He was the only one not to have said anything and she wondered why. Ah well, it would all come out soon enough. She tucked into her dinner, savouring the tender turkey breast and hoping Margaret would pack plenty up for them to take home. They could enjoy a nice turkey sarnie tonight as well as Bella having a dinner.

*

Bella stirred as she heard the front door opening and voices in the hallway. The bedroom was dark; she sat up for a moment, confused, wondering why she had her coat and scarf on and was lying on her bed. Then she remembered. She'd left Bobby's home in a hurry. And she remembered why. Her mam was calling her, so she slid off the bed and opened the door, peering down the stairs at her mam's flushed face.

'Ah, there you are, chuck. Are you okay?'

Bella shrugged and walked slowly down the stairs. She took off her coat and scarf and hung them on the hall pegs. 'I think so,

Mam.' Her lips trembled and Mam put her arms around her and held her close. 'It's just been a funny day, hasn't it? I'd rather have Christmas in our own house.'

'So would I, chuck, but we didn't half get well looked after. Fenella is a good hostess, I'll give her that.'

'That's because she does bugger all else but give orders,' Dad said. 'She's got plenty of time to play at being her ladyship.'

'Oh get away with you, Harry; I didn't see you refusing anything, food nor drinks.'

'Well I'd have been a bloody fool to, now wouldn't I? Grub as good as that doesn't often pass my lips.'

Bella started to laugh and then they were all chuckling together. When they finally recovered she said, 'What are you both like? Well at least you enjoyed it. What about you, Molly?'

Her sister nodded. 'I wanted to stay and play some board games with Bobby but Mam insisted we come back because she told them you were feeling poorly and that she'd sent you home.'

Bella's eyes widened. 'Did you, Mam? And what did Bobby say to that?'

'Not a lot. He was quiet all the time and just toyed with his food. You need to have a chat with him, chuck, try and find out if he is involved with the young girl they mentioned. If he is, maybe he didn't feel it was right to bring it up with you. After all, like you are always saying, you're just good pals and nothing more. He might think that's all you want to be. If you don't, then a good talk will soon put that right.'

Bella shrugged. 'We'll see. I'm seeing Fran and Edie tomorrow. I'll see what they think. Can I have some of the food you brought home? I'm starving.' She wanted to think about something else; otherwise it would go on all night.

If Bobby did have a girl – and his family seemed to think he did – then what was the point in harbouring any feelings other than friendship for him? They could still sing, just as they'd been doing before Alicia's name had even been mentioned. And Bobby had denied what his mother had said. So who knew what was going on?

*

Fran shook her head after Bella's departing back. She looked at Edie, who shrugged. Their friend had just told them all about her Christmas Day upset during the threesome's usual Boxing Day morning walk over The Mystery with Edie's little fox terrier, Rebel.

'What do you make of that then?' Fran asked, sitting down on a wooden bench. She pulled her woollen scarf tightly around her neck and tucked her hands under her armpits to keep them warm. She'd forgotten to bring her gloves out with her and her hands were freezing.

'Not sure,' Edie said, sitting down beside her and pulling Rebel close to her legs. 'It sounds almost like his mother thinks he'll marry the girl eventually; like the family expects it.'

'Hmm, like them arranged marriages you hear about for foreign people. You'd think he'd have said something to his mum though while Bella was there, even if he only said it in a joking sort of way, so that his mum gets the idea he doesn't want to be with whatsername. It must have really upset Bella for her to run off like that. She's obviously got more feelings for him than she's letting on.'

Edie nodded. 'What about our singing? She's got to talk to him about that hasn't she?'

'Well we're back in work tomorrow, so we'll have a discussion about it at dinnertime. And if she still wants to do it then we'll tell our parents and maybe have a chat with Bobby as well.'

'I hope my mam says yes,' Edie said. 'I'd love to get out of the factory for good one day.'

'Me too.'

*

Bella rounded the corner of Victory Street to see a familiar figure standing at her front door, his hand raised as though about to knock on the door. The house was empty as her mam and dad had taken Molly to see an uncle in Old Swan. He turned as she approached and his wary smile made her heart beat a little faster. But she tried to keep her voice level as she said, 'Bobby. What do you want?'

'Bella, I need to talk to you. About what happened yesterday.'

'You'd better come inside,' she said, unlocking the door and leading the way into the back room. 'Sit down and I'll make us a hot drink. I've been out walking with Fran and Edie and I'm freezing.'

He sat on the sofa while she busied herself making two mugs of steaming tea and carried them into the room. She handed one to him and then sat down on her dad's chair at the side of the fireplace.

'Thank you,' he said, putting his mug down on the coffee table next to a half-finished jigsaw puzzle of a sandy cove, blue sea and cliffs, one of Molly's Christmas presents. 'Look, I'm really sorry about yesterday. Your mother said she'd sent you home, but I kind of got the impression that you'd already gone.'

She nodded and looked at the floor. 'I had.'

'Because of what Mother said about me and Alicia?'

'*Is* there a you and Alicia?'

He shook his head. 'Not in the way you think. To me, Alicia is like the sister I never had. Our parents were the best of friends and we were practically brought up together. We're as close as siblings. Our mothers always talked about how lovely it would be if we married each other eventually and our families were related, but believe me, it will never happen. I don't feel that sort of love for her, just brotherly love, that's all. But Mum's still got this idea in her head.'

Bella took a sip of her tea and peered from under her fringe at him. 'I overreacted, I think.'

He gave her a tentative smile. 'But was that because you care or don't care? I know that you're angry with me, but there's no need. I never even thought to mention Alicia because it was never relevant to any of our conversations, not because I was trying to hide something from you.'

Bella sighed and put down her mug. 'Probably because I *do* care,' she admitted. 'But I'm scared of caring for someone who doesn't care back.'

He went to kneel beside her chair. 'Bella, I do care, I care very much. You have become the most important thing in my life – you and our singing together are all I live for. In fact, I'm pretty sure I've fallen in love with you.'

Bella stared at him. 'In love with me?' she repeated.

He nodded. 'Yes,' he whispered. 'Oh I know we're ridiculously young and there's a war looming and we don't know what's going to happen next, but yes, I really do love you. What about you. How do you feel about me?'

She put her hands up to her mouth, feeling more shocked than she'd ever felt about anything, and realised that yes, she did – love him, that is.

She reached out to stroke his cheek and he caught her hand and held it to his lips. She took a deep breath and burst out, 'Yes, Bobby, I love you too.'

He pulled her to her feet and into his arms. They shared their first real kiss, then drew apart and looked into each other's eyes. 'Oh my God,' he said. 'I see it in your eyes – I've seen it before when we were singing, but I never realised what it was. I do now. I love you, and it feels so good to say it.'

'I love you too, I really do. And it feels so right to say it.'

They sat down together on the sofa and Bobby held her tight in his arms. Bella didn't want to move as he kissed her time and again, but when they heard the front door opening they sprang hurriedly apart and Bella straightened her hair and her dress where Bobby's hands had roamed.

'Let's tell them about the singing at the club,' he whispered before Bella's parents came into the room. 'Then that's another thing out of the way.'

She laughed and squeezed his hand. 'So I was a thing, was I? Okay, well at least we're making some progress now.' The door opened and she got up to greet her mam and dad. 'Where's Molly?' she asked.

'At her pal's down the street,' Mam replied. 'Oh hello, Bobby. Fancy seeing you here.'

Bobby smiled. 'Yes, we've been talking and sorting some things out,' he said. 'Err, will it be okay with you both if Bella and I did a bit of courting from time to time?'

Mam's face broke into a wide grin. 'Well it is with me, son. Harry, what about you? Is it all right if Bobby takes our Bella out now and again?'

'Aye, lad. Be my guest,' Dad said, shaking Bobby by the hand. 'As long as you look after her, it's fine by Mary and me.'

'There's one more thing we need to talk about,' Bella said, nodding at Bobby, who joined in. They explained about the offer from Chas Morris and how they really wanted to give it a try.

'Harry, what do you think?' Mam asked. 'I'm okay if you are.'

Dad nodded. 'It's not every day this sort of chance comes your way,' he said. 'Take it while you can, we don't know what's around the corner in the next few months. Enjoy yourselves and go and do it.'

Bella flung her arms around both of her parents. 'Thank you so much. We'll make you proud one day.'

'We already are, chuck,' her dad said and he shook Bobby by the hand. 'Good luck to you two and to the Bryant Sisters as well. May you all have every success that you deserve.'

Chapter Twelve

April 1940

By the time Bella's sixteenth birthday had come and gone the country was in a state of flux. According to regular reports on the wireless and her dad's daily *Echo* headlines, and even though he'd declared war on Germany last year, Neville Chamberlain was showing signs of being ill-equipped to save Europe from Nazi conquest. There were calls for him to give up his Conservative Party leadership and let Winston Churchill take the helm.

Bella didn't fully understand what her dad was going on about night after night when he was reading his paper and ranting on about the disgraceful way things were being managed. There had been attacks on ships crossing the Atlantic with supplies of goods and food and Dad said did that bugger Hitler want them all to starve, because that's what would happen if something didn't change soon.

Mam was complaining about the shortages in the shops. Ration books had been issued in January and bacon, butter and sugar were now in short supply, along with many other goods. Things at work had taken a strange turn too. Most of the single lads on the factory floor had signed up for the forces, leaving the women behind to hold the fort.

Fran's little brother Alfie had been evacuated to a farm in North Wales, but Mam still refused to let Molly go, even though Molly had told her that half of her class had gone to families in Wales and were enjoying themselves and there was loads more to eat there than in Liverpool. Fran's two older brothers had joined the army, ignoring their mother's protests.

'My brother Don said the war will be over by Christmas anyway,' Fran announced one morning, as they waited for the tram to take them to work. 'But he said they might as well as go and do their bit to get it finished quicker. My Frankie is going next week and he's to be billeted in Yorkshire somewhere for now. I don't mind him being in the army and he did look so smart in his uniform, but what if they decide to send them away to France? It looks awful over there, like a proper war zone. That scares the life out of me.'

Bella squeezed her arm as a tram came trundling into view. 'He'll be fine and like your Don says, it'll all be over and done with soon.' She hoped it would, as Bobby did nothing but talk about joining the RAF now he was nearly seventeen. His father was supposed to be sorting it all out for him. He wouldn't be able to fly planes yet but he could be carted off in one to God knew where.

At the match factory the mood wasn't much better and two of the women on the packing line were grumbling about their sons leaving home. 'Don't know how I'm supposed to manage without his wages. I've two more mouths to feed as well as pay me rent and put money in the meters,' the woman called Marge said.

Her friend Patti agreed. 'Yes, it's always us women that suffer when these bloody wars start. I remember how me poor old mam, God rest her soul, struggled when we was little and our dad was away fighting. And he never came back. It's always bloody men start it and us women what's left behind holding the babbies and expected to deal with everything. And another thing, having to remember to cart them bloody gas mask boxes everywhere we go.'

'Well, you've still got your 'usband at home,' Marge said, winding her turban around her head and tying it in a neat knot at the front. 'Can't he get a few more hours down at the docks? And that gas mask might save your life one day; you never know when you'll need it.'

'I suppose he can try and get more hours, but he was talking about "doing his bit" last night as well. I'm going to have to send me kids away. It's the only thing I can think of doing right now that makes any sense. How's your Alfie getting on, Fran? Has he settled in okay with his new family?'

Fran smiled. 'As far as we know. We had a short letter last week and he seemed fine and liked the cakes the farmer's wife makes. At least we know he's safe now, just in case.'

'And is your mam still refusing to send Molly away?' Marge asked Bella. 'She could always go with her you know. A few have done that and they help out on the farms they are staying at. Makes sense to me. I wouldn't mind giving it a go myself.'

Bella sighed. 'I can't see Mam doing that, well not right now anyway. We'll have to see what happens.'

At break time the threesome sat hugging mugs of tea, the gloomy atmosphere settling on everyone's shoulders. There were no wisecracks from the young lads to make them all smile. They were sadly missed and the main workforce was all women, who could talk about nothing but rationing and evacuation. It felt depressing.

Fran got to her feet. 'Come on, I've had enough of this doom and gloom. Song time,' she announced, standing on a chair to get attention. Bella and Edie jumped up and joined in with Fran's rendition of 'Alexander's Ragtime Band'. By the time the song came to an end everyone was smiling and thanking the girls for cheering them up.

'At least we've got our nights out singing at Speke Legion to give us a bit of a break from it all,' Eddie said. 'Thank God. I wish we could do more than just once a month though.'

'Me too,' Bella said. 'But we might get more bookings soon because some of the variety acts are male and most are young enough to be called up. Which means we ladies will be there to fill in the slots left by them.'

'Hmm, now there's a thought, Bella,' Fran said. 'But we'll have hardly any audience if the younger blokes are away. Anyway, we'll have to see, won't we?'

*

On Friday 10 May Neville Chamberlain stepped down from his post and Winston Churchill was appointed prime minister of the United Kingdom.

'And not before time,' Dad said from his usual chair by the fire as Bella, her mam and Molly were sitting around the table finishing their tea, the wireless giving regular updates in the background. 'With Churchill in charge we stand a chance of defeating bloody Hitler once and for all.'

He flicked his ash onto the tiled hearth, earning him a look of disapproval from his wife, and carried on. 'We really do need to think seriously about letting our Molly go somewhere safer, Mary. It's selfish to keep her here, because I'll tell you now; things are going to start hotting up. You might find yourself in an air raid while at work and Bella won't be here either, then what? Molly will have to go down the cellar on her own for God knows how long. What if a bomb falls on the house, or on Olive Mount when you're working?'

Mam frowned at him. 'Well if I'm working at night, you'll be home, and she can always knock on next door if she's worried.'

Dad fidgeted in his chair, a sheepish air about him. Bella frowned.

'Dad, what have you been up to?' She knew even before he admitted it that he'd signed up. Suddenly she didn't want any more tea and her stomach felt like it had fallen down three flights of stairs. *Not Dad too.*

'I've, er, well I've enlisted today. I'll be leaving the trams next week and joining the army. No, Mary,' he said as she jumped to her feet and began to protest that he was too old. 'I'm not too old at all, and they need every man they can get. If we want a peaceful world for our kids to inherit, we need to fight for it with everything we've got.'

'And what about us? We need you Harry. I can't lose you too,' said Mam, starting to cry.

Dad tried to stay practical. 'I'll get paid as a soldier. You'll still get your housekeeping money and what have you. If Molly is evacuated the government pay for her keep and that will save a bit as well. *And* she'll be safer.'

Mary chewed on her lip, taking big gulps of air. 'Molly, what do you have to say about this, chuck?'

Molly shrugged but her voice started to crack. 'Whatever you think is best. If it makes it easier, I'll g-go. And then there's only you and Bella to worry about, Mam.'

Bella reached for her mam and sister's hands, giving them a squeeze. 'Mam, we're not the only family in Liverpool that's got to do this,' she said. 'Everybody we know is either sending their little ones to safety or the men and older boys are joining up.'

Mam sat back down, tears in her eyes again. 'I feel like I'm losing my family one by one here. This was not how I saw my life panning out.' She took a deep breath and tried to smile. 'That bleedin' Hitler. If I ever get my hands on him, he'll rue the day he was born.'

'You and the rest of us, gel. Get in the queue,' Dad said. 'We'll have one more weekend as normal as we can and then on Monday we'll get Molly sorted out, and make sure that cellar is as safe and as comfortable as it can be. I've a feeling you'll be spending a fair bit of time down there.'

*

The last Saturday in May, Bobby held Bella tight as he kissed her goodbye on the platform at Lime Street station. He looked so smart in his blue air force uniform and her heart thumped hard as he looked into her eyes. He was travelling to the Brize Norton base in Oxfordshire, where he was joining his father, who had resumed his position as a wing commander. She was conscious of his mother and the girl Alicia, who had been brought to live with the Harrison family while her father spent the last few weeks of his life in a sanatorium, staring at them.

'I'll write to you,' he whispered to Bella. 'Please write back as often as you can. I love you.'

'I will,' she whispered back. 'I love you too. I'd better let those two say their goodbyes now. If looks could kill,' she added, feeling Alicia's eyes burning into her back. 'Stay safe, please.'

'I'll do my best. And if I get any time off, I'll be right back to see you.'

She swallowed hard and backed away so that his mother and Alicia could say their farewells. His mother came back to stand beside Bella, sobbing. Alicia's piping voice carried loud and clear over the noise and hustle and bustle of the station as people said goodbye to their loved ones.

'Darling Robert,' she simpered. 'Keep yourself safe for me. I promise to write every day until you're back home with us, your family.' She emphasised the 'your family' as though Bella meant nothing and, tossing her long blonde hair over her shoulders, she flung herself at him so hard he nearly fell backwards onto a couple of squaddies who were strolling past with their kit bags slung on their backs.

'Steady on, mate,' one of them joked. 'Lucky you,' said the other.

Bobby looked embarrassed, his cheeks flushed pink, and he gave a final wave and hurried away down the platform along with a crowd of soldiers and airmen. Alicia joined Bobby's mother and Bella noticed the sly look in the girl's eyes. Alicia slipped her arm through Fenella's and said, 'Don't worry Aunty Fen, we'll look after one another while our menfolk look after our country.'

Bella felt angry – Bobby was *her* manfolk – but she wasn't getting into an argument here with the girl. She'd been told a few weeks ago that Alicia was staying at Bobby's for the foreseeable future, and she now wondered what they'd talked about on nights she wasn't seeing him, which, apart from the choir nights and the singing at the Legion, hadn't been all that often lately with the way things were.

'Of course we will, darling,' Fenella assured her. 'We'll be just like mother and daughter while they're away.'

Alicia's smug smile was more than Bella could bear and she waved them goodbye and hurried to jump on a bus outside the station while they waited for the car to pick them up. Bobby's father had hired a driver who was exempt from war duties as he was too elderly. All right for some, Bella thought as she took a seat upstairs on the crowded bus. They could have offered her a lift as they were going so close to Victory Street.

Her mind played tricks all the way home and by the time she got off the bus she'd convinced herself that Bobby wouldn't write, he'd just said that because she'd expect it, and he would come home when the war was over and marry Alicia, like his mother so obviously wanted. She hammered on Fran's door and when Fran let her in she burst into tears. Fran led her through to the back room, where Edie was sitting at the table cradling a mug of tea in her hands.

'Where is everyone?' Bella sobbed, looking round.

'Granny's asleep in the front room, Mam's at the shops and Dad and the boys are all away, of course. Me and Edie were just having a natter.' She peered at Bella. 'Right, what's up? Oh, I know, you've been to wave Bobby off haven't you. Bless you; he'll be okay, just like my Frankie will. He'll write as soon as he can.'

Bella bawled her eyes out at that and told Fran and Edie what had happened at Lime Street station.

'Well the devious little cow,' Fran said. 'How dare she and right in front of his girl as well. I'd have slapped her face.'

'I might have been tempted if his mother hadn't been there. After they said their goodbyes I didn't get the chance to say anything else to him as he was getting on his train. It was packed down there, so many of our boys going away. I don't have a good feeling about it at all, Fran.'

'He'll be fine, Bella,' Edie reassured her. 'He's not going to be flying planes for a good while anyway; he'll be more likely to be on lookout duties around the area. But at least he'll feel he's doing something to help. And he'll write, you know he will.' She poured Bella a mug of tea and handed it to her. 'Get that down you while it's hot.'

'Thank you.' Bella sighed and took a sip. 'I know he won't be flying, but that doesn't mean it'll be all ground work for him. He'll be taken up to fly with others, no doubt, and I can't help worrying.'

Edie shook her head. 'Not a lot we can do about it but wait. And sing. Don't forget, we've got the extra night at the Legion next week, Friday and Saturday. Something to look forward to at least. We'll get a bit of practice in this week and it will help take our minds off other things for a while.'

Chapter Thirteen

August 1940

With Dad somewhere miles away and Molly safely evacuated to North Wales, it was just Bella and her mam who dashed down to the cellar as the air raid siren sounded, wailing loud and clear.

This was the fifth night in succession that their sleep had been disturbed. Bella felt weary and the camp beds were uncomfortable, but so far their street had been safe. Nearby Stevenson Street had taken a hit in a big way. Several houses had been destroyed and deaths and many casualties reported. It brought it home to them that this was all too real and they couldn't take a chance and stay in bed, because Victory Street might be next. At least down in the cellar they could light a couple of candles, and they'd made a flask of tea just in case, before they'd turned in for the night.

'What's that noise?' Bella whispered, once they were tucked up the best they could. She could hear a scratching noise and the hairs on the back of her neck rose. 'Oh my God, is it a mouse?' She drew her legs up and wrapped a blanket around herself.

Mam cocked her ear and then shook her head. 'It's outside. Probably one of the ARP wardens doing a check to make sure everywhere is dark. Sounds like boots scraping on concrete to me.

Perhaps he's stood in dog muck or something and is trying to clean his boot on the edge of the pavement.'

Bella breathed a sigh of relief and tried to relax. She tossed and turned and gave up on sleep as a bad job, her mind going over the events of the last few weeks. Her last letter from Bobby was safely stashed away in her handbag and that was lying beside her camp bed, but the others he'd sent were upstairs in her bedside drawers. If a bomb fell on the house they'd be destroyed. She thought about going and getting them, but she could hear the drone of planes as they circled the area.

Ear-splitting thuds sounded, making her jump, and she wondered who'd copped for *those* particular bombs. Half of the city had been badly damaged already; many of the city centre shops and businesses had been hit, whole streets of houses down near the dock, churches, schools, and row after row of tenements in the poorer inner-city area.

It seemed the Germans would keep on until they'd flattened the lot. Fran hadn't heard from Frankie for over five weeks and was frantic with worry. He'd been sent to France last month and his last letter had been posted before he left England. Bella and Edie tried their best to keep her spirits up, but it was hard to keep cheerful with so much uncertainty. Nearly every shift at the factory had been interrupted by an air raid warning and even though some had been false alarms, they still had to hurry along to the shelters.

Bella still picked up a copy of the *Liverpool Echo* on her way home from work. She felt closer to her dad when she could see a copy on the dining table. She'd read tonight that terrible things were happening to Jewish people in a place built by the Germans in occupied Poland. The place was named Auschwitz and was being called a concentration camp by the newspaper reporters. People were being herded like sheep into the camp and reports claimed that thousands had been killed by being gassed to death just simply for the fact they were Jewish.

Liverpool had a big Jewish community, many of whom owned the local businesses. Bella hoped that the Germans wouldn't come rounding up people from their own city. The whole nightmare of this war seemed never-ending.

She turned on her side, nearly tipping the camp bed over, and prayed for the all-clear warning. Mam was already asleep, snoring gently, after her long day at Olive Mount Hospital. They'd had injured military staff brought in as well as the sick children they usually nursed. She'd worked extra hours to help get unused rooms and wards cleaned and ready for the new patients, and had been shattered when she came home from work.

Eventually, feeling her eyes closing, Bella gave in and drifted off to sleep. Her dreams were as explosive as the bombs falling on her city and several times she awoke with a jump, thinking she could hear footsteps in the rooms above. 'Hurry up, morning,' she muttered.

Finally she heard the faint wailing of the all-clear sirens. She got up quietly, picked up her handbag and crept up the cellar steps. Mam would go mad if she woke her up and she hoped the door wouldn't creak too loudly. She took a peep around the downstairs rooms but all seemed intact, although it was pretty dark with no lights showing anywhere. Upstairs, she luxuriated in the double bed that was all hers now and then felt immediately guilty that her sisters weren't with her. She closed her eyes and fell asleep within seconds.

When the girls arrived at work the following morning they were all told to assemble in the canteen, where hot tea and plates of buttered toast were waiting for them. Everyone took a seat. George Barratt, the foreman, stood at the top end of the room and asked for silence as he had an announcement to make.

He cleared his throat and began. 'I'm afraid I have some very bad news to relate. Last night, our other factory in Litherland was completely destroyed by bombs. Several members of our night shift were killed. Needless to say this is a tragedy and our thoughts and sympathy go out to their families. Today we will close this site as a mark of respect. I know that many of you knew staff down there and some of you are also related. Finish your teas, go home, and stay safe and I'll see you tomorrow, all being well.'

'Blimey,' Fran said, shaking her head. 'Well, that puts moaning about the ration books and gas masks into perspective.'

'It does indeed,' Edie agreed. 'Oh God, this is awful. Some of the girls that went on nights a while back used to work alongside us here. It doesn't bear thinking about.'

Bella took a deep breath. 'And I did nothing but grumble to myself last night because I had disturbed sleep. I feel consumed with guilt now.'

'We all moaned,' Fran said. 'So don't feel too bad about it.'

Bella nodded wearily. 'Shall we all go back to mine? Mam's at work, we'll have the place to ourselves. We could do some rehearsing for the weekend. Cheer us up a bit. Maybe learn a new song or two.'

Fran sighed and finished her tea. 'Come on then, sup up. Let's go. It's not often we get a day off midweek.'

As they jumped from the tram near The Mystery Park a sudden thought struck Bella. 'Will you come to Bobby's house with me please? I just want to see if they're okay and if they've had any letters recently. It's been over two weeks since I last had one and he usually writes at least once a week. I'm presuming he's still in Oxfordshire, but who knows.'

The threesome linked arms and strode across the park. Apart from the stench of burning in the air and plumes of smoke in the distance, the day was warm and bright and quite pleasant. Bella knocked on the door of Bobby's house and stepped back, rocking on her heels. Eventually the door was opened and Margaret stood there, her uniform as crisp as on the Christmas Day they'd been invited to dinner.

She smiled, but didn't seem to recognise Bella. 'Yes, ladies, can I help you?'

'Is Mrs Harrison at home, please? Bella asked, chewing her lip nervously.

'I'm sorry, dear. Mrs Harrison and Miss Alicia are away in Oxfordshire. They went last week and are staying with friends for the foreseeable future. Wing Commander Harrison and young Master Robert are stationed in that area so it made sense for the rest of the family to stay down there. I believe it's safer as they are out in the country. Whom shall I say called, if Mrs Harrison rings later?'

'Err, well I'm Bobby, err Robert's girlfriend, Bella. I met you at Christmas, Margaret.'

Margaret peered short-sightedly at her. 'Ah, yes, I recognise you now, miss. The young lady that was taken ill at Christmas lunchtime. Very well, I'll let them know.'

Bella nodded. 'I just wondered if they'd heard from Robert lately, that's all.'

'Well, a couple of letters arrived on Saturday and I'll forward them on. One for Mrs Harrison and the other one for Miss Alicia, both in young Mr Robert's handwriting.'

'Thank you.' Bella felt like she'd been punched in the stomach. So, he could find the time to write to bloody Alicia and his mother, but not to her. And he was still in England – letters only took a couple of days to arrive, even with a war on. If there was nothing for her when she got home, she would write to him tonight and give him a piece of her mind.

Back at Bella's house the girls sat at the table and listed all the songs they knew, including the ones that Bobby had sung with Bella. There wasn't much else they could come up with and Fran shook her head. 'So many of the popular songs are instrumentals and not something we could do. Let's hope the songwriters get their acts together and write some more for the Andrews Sisters because those sort of songs with the split harmonies suit us to a T.'

Bella sighed and got up to put the kettle on. There'd been no letter from Bobby waiting for her on the doormat, just one from Molly in a fancy pink envelope, and she'd put that on the sideboard until Mam got in from work and they could read it together. It was a pity Bobby hadn't been posted to a closer airbase; then they at least could have met up occasionally.

She'd bet a penny to a pound that he was meeting up with blooming Alicia from time to time now she was down there. Well, she wasn't going to waste time crying over him. She'd write him one more letter tonight and if he hadn't answered her in two weeks then she would put him out of her mind and concentrate on the Bryant Sisters and trying to survive this war in one piece.

She brewed a pot of tea and poured three mugs. 'Fancy a sarnie?' she shouted through to the sitting room. 'We've not got much in but there's a pot of fish paste in the cupboard.'

'I'll have one,' Edie said, but Fran pulled a face.

'Not for me, thanks. Not keen on fish. Makes me feel sick.'

'What about tomatoes then? There's a couple on Dad's plant by the back door.'

'Oh go on then. Put me plenty of salt on though.'

Bella laughed and set to slicing yesterday's loaf. 'Do you want a bit of tomato on with your paste, Edie?'

'Yeah, why not. Let's live dangerously for once.'

Fran carried the plates of sandwiches through on a tray along with the mugs of tea. 'We'll have these and then we'll get some rehearsing done. I do wish we had a piano. But we'll manage. We've done it before with no one accompanying us. Tuck in.'

On Saturday night, the crowd in the Legion cheered and clapped loudly as the girls took a bow following their first half of the show.

Chas Morris saw them offstage and told the audience they'd be back later to finish the evening with a dancing spot. He announced a game of lotto and the ticket seller set up a table and chairs in front of the stage, where a queue formed immediately.

As the girls left their dressing room Chas called them over to a table, where a glass jug of orange squash and three glasses waited. They flopped down on the chairs around the table and Edie poured drinks for them all.

'God, I needed that,' Bella said. 'It's so warm in here tonight. My throat's as dry as a bone.'

'Well done, girls, that was great,' Chas said. 'How are things at work? I heard about the other site. Dreadful. Makes you wonder when it's all going to end.'

Fran nodded. 'A couple of girls we used to work with were killed. It's so very sad. They'd volunteered for night shifts there thinking it would help their families out with the bit of extra pay they'd get. And that's what happens. It's so unfair.'

'It is,' Chas agreed. 'Well I might have something nice happening for you next weekend. I won't say anything yet in case it falls through. But just in case, come early to get the sound right. Dress as glamorous as you can afford to and give the performance of your life. I promise you it will be worth it, all being well that Hitler doesn't wipe us out first. Right, I'll go and call the lotto numbers and I'll see you later.'

Bella looked at the others, her eyebrows raised. 'Wonder what that's all about then?

'No idea,' Fran said. 'But whatever it is, it'll take our minds off worrying about Bobby and Frankie.'

Nails painted, hair styled into immaculate waves and their dresses as neatly pressed as was possible, Bella and the girls flung their hearts and souls into the final song of their first spot. 'Apple Blossom Time' was always a popular song to end a first spot with. The pianist pounded the keys and a saxophone-playing mate of Chas's had been brought in tonight to swell the backing. As they took a bow and Chas got up onstage to thank them, the audience went wild, cheering, clapping and shouting, 'More!'

'You'll get more later,' Chas announced, smiling gleefully, as the girls trooped offstage and into the dressing room. He went to the bar and got their usual jug of squash and took it over to a table where a smartly dressed man sat on his own, smoking a cigar. 'What did you think?' he asked.

'Spot on,' the man replied. 'Exactly what I'm looking for.'

'I thought that might be the case.' Chas nodded. 'I'll be sorry to see them go, but I'd never stand in their way.'

'They haven't said yes yet,' the man said as the girls came across to the table, all smiles and waving at people they recognised.

'They will,' Chas said confidently. 'Girls,' he addressed them. 'Take a seat. I'd like to introduce you to a pal of mine, Basil Jenkins. Baz, mate, this is Bella, Fran and Edie, otherwise known as the Bryant Sisters. I'll leave you three in Basil's capable hands while I go and do the lotto. See you later.'

Bella smiled. 'Nice to meet you, Mr Jenkins.'

'Basil, please,' he said, shaking her outstretched hand. 'And it's nice to meet you three as well. Tell me a little about yourselves and how you came to form the Bryant Sisters act.'

'Well,' Bella began. 'We started singing in the school choir years ago and always sang in church.'

'And then Bella won a Maia Choir scholarship,' Fran took over. 'Along with her friend Bobby, and they did festivals and shows and then we started singing at work to keep people's spirits up and our foreman invited Chas to the Christmas do and announced us as the Bryant Sisters.'

'That's cos we work at the match factory, Bryant & May's,' Edie continued. 'And that's it really; it's how it all started. Chas asked if we'd do some shows for him, and here we are.'

'And here you are, indeed,' Basil agreed. 'And may I say what a polished and professional show you ladies put on.'

'You're not from Liverpool, are you?' Fran said. 'That accent sounds a bit too posh for up here.' She reached for the squash jug and poured herself a drink. She filled the other glasses and gestured with the jug towards Basil, but he declined and held up a tumbler with what looked like whisky in it.

'Kent,' he said. 'Tunbridge Wells. I'm visiting family living on the Wirral. I've known Chas for a number of years and I always pop in to see him when I'm up this way. I've driven in through the centre of the city, dear Lord what a mess. But London is the same. Such devastation everywhere you go.' As Basil finished speaking, the familiar loud wailing of the air raid warnings sirens sounded and an angry woman jumped to her feet.

'Bleedin' 'itler. I only wanted two more numbers for a full house on me lotto card,' she yelled. 'I'll swing for 'im.'

'Me and you both, Nellie,' her friend said, picking up her coat and handbag from the seat next to her. 'Come on, queen, let's go get in that shelter.'

Chas, Basil and the girls huddled together at the bottom end of the shelter in the grounds of the Legion. As planes droned overhead and bombs whistled down on parts of Liverpool that really didn't need any more, Basil said, 'I didn't get a chance to talk properly before Hitler put his oar in, but I'm really impressed with your act, ladies, and I've got a proposition to make. I'm currently scouting the country for top-class entertainers like yourselves. I work for ENSA, which I'm sure you've heard of.'

All three nodded. They had indeed heard of ENSA and thought it sounded an exciting life. The Entertainments National Service Association was proving popular. It had been set up to provide entertainment for recruited servicemen in and around their base camps and help to keep up morale.

'I'll keep it short but sweet seeing as we're stuck in here, but I'd like to sign up the Bryant Sisters. How does that sound?' He sat back on the narrow bench seat as they all stared at him.

'Us? You want to sign us up?' Fran asked. 'What, you mean to travel with other acts and what have you, like proper entertainers?' Bella was speechless and Edie wide-eyed.

'That's about it, yes,' Basil replied. 'I realise you're all very young and I'm happy to make appointments with your parents to discuss the matter. Oh, and you'll need to give up your jobs. But we'll pay you well, feed you and you'll be billeted wherever we are appearing. Might not be the Ritz, but the places I've visited are clean, dry and as warm as can be expected. We'll provide you with stage clothes and maybe military uniforms for travelling. What do you say?'

The girls were all speechless. Edie's mouth was actually hanging open.

Basil laughed. 'I can see you're all shocked, but we'll have another chat when we can get back inside and I'll look forward to the second half of your show later.'

Chapter Fourteen

Mary Rogers, Fran's mam Vera Jackson and Edie's mam Doris Potts sat around the table at Bella's house. Basil sat in the fourth chair, outlining his plans and trying to reassure the worried ladies that he would do everything he possibly could to take care of their daughters, who were in the front room, anxiously awaiting the parental decision. He assured them that he would make sure they were chaperoned at all times.

'It really is a wonderful opportunity for them and they are so talented,' he said. 'They are England's answer to the Andrews Sisters. They are going to be so popular, big stars. It would be a shame to rob them of this chance to earn a decent living doing something they enjoy in such an uncertain time. We all need to grab happiness where we can, don't you agree?'

The mothers looked at each and nodded.

Mary sighed. 'Well, apart from missing her terribly, the only thing for me is losing Bella's wages. I need them to keep a roof over our heads. Well, mine at least, if she goes. All my family will be away, apart from my youngest that passed away...' She tailed off and wiped away a tear that had trickled down her cheek.

'I'm sorry to hear that,' Basil said. 'About your little one, I mean. The girls will be paid a good wage; we'll feed and clothe them. They'll be able to send money home. You'll all have one less mouth to feed. Every little helps.'

'Mary, you can always stay with me if you feel a bit lonely,' Vera said.

'And me,' Doris said. 'Vera and me are a bit tied because we've got the oldies to see to. At least you've only yourself to think about at the moment, Mary, and it'd be nice for us to have a bit of company.'

Mary nodded. 'So shall we call them in and tell them, then? I feel that proud, but sad at the same time. They'll be doing their bit for the war effort, but in a nicer way than usual. They're lucky girls to get this chance. You go and bring them through, Basil. You're the boss now.'

Basil smiled and got to his feet. He tapped on the front room door, opened it and peered inside. The girls looked at him with worried expressions. They'd all voiced concerns that they wouldn't be allowed to join ENSA. But Basil wasn't about to let a golden opportunity like these three pass him by. They were good-looking girls and the fact he'd got a brown-eyed brunette, a green-eyed redhead – well auburn, anyway – and a blue-eyed blonde was amazing. The Andrews Sisters were all of very similar colouring, but his girls were striking and unusual and he was certain they would attract a following wherever they played. He couldn't wait to try them with a big backing band.

'Come on through,' he said, trying to keep a straight face and give nothing away as all three stared at him with questioning expressions from the sofa where they were huddled together.

They jumped to their feet and followed him through to the back, each one holding their breath.

'Tell them, Basil,' Mary said, looking at the girls, whose eyes were nearly popping out of their heads. 'Put them out of their misery.'

Basil laughed. 'Girls, you can relax, it's a yes from your mothers.'

They squealed and jumped around the room, hugging each other and their mams and Basil.

'Group hug,' Basil said, enveloping the lot of them.

They all hugged each other tightly.

Basil laughed. 'Right, sit down and we'll talk business. I'll need you to sign a contract and your mams to sign it too, to show they give their permission for you to be a part of the ENSA team.'

'And I'll make a fresh pot of tea,' Mary said. 'It helps keep Liverpool afloat.'

*

During the usual air raid, when Bella thought it must surely be their turn for a bomb – they expected it every night when the German planes flew low overhead – she and her mam, down in the cellar, talked long into the night.

'I'm going to miss you, chuck, I really am,' Mam said. 'I don't know. Life's so strange. I go from a houseful of family to nothing, almost overnight. I'll write to your dad tomorrow and tell him what's happening. He'll be so proud of you. And I'll write to our Molly as well.'

'I've written a quick letter to Bobby, but he still hasn't answered the last two that I sent him. So if he doesn't answer the next one then I'm just going to put him to the back of my mind and get on with my life. There'll be time enough to catch up when we get back to normal, whatever that is these days.'

'He might just be really busy, chuck; bet he's not had a minute to himself. I bet none of them have. Has Fran heard from Frankie yet?'

Bella shook her head. 'No, and neither has his mam, but he's abroad so he's got a good excuse, I suppose. As far as I know and I have been told by Margaret at the Harrisons', Bobby is still in Oxfordshire. I told you his mother and that Alicia one are down there now as well didn't I?'

'You did, love. But that doesn't mean anything. Just be patient. There's a war on.'

'Oh, really?' Bella giggled half-heartedly. 'I hadn't noticed.'

*

George the foreman called the girls into his office first thing the following morning. 'Chas has been on the blower with the good news that his mate Basil has signed you up,' he told them. 'Congratulations. What a wonderful opportunity for you all. Get out of this city while you still can.'

'Thank you, George,' said Bella. 'And for giving us our name – we'll always be the Bryant Sisters. I just hope there's a Bryant & May's to come back to when all of this is over.'

'You and me both, queen. I'm terrified they'll bomb this factory now they've done the Litherland one. I know the war's not confined to just us here, but you might be safer in smaller places and the military bases are not as obvious to the planes, and they're well-manned, so attack is less likely on them. Enjoy yourselves, have the best time, stay close to one another and watch out for them randy soldiers. Just behave and you'll be fine. Work the rest of the week on notice and then you'll be off. I envy you girls, I really do. Give us a few songs before you leave on our dinner breaks and keep 'em all cheerful.'

On Friday dinnertime the girls were led blindfolded into the canteen, where in spite of rationing, a beautiful cake took pride of place, GOOD LUCK piped across the white icing in big pink letters. Plates of sarnies and home-made sausage rolls were handed out and everyone tucked in.

When the tables were cleared the girls got up to sing the only appropriate song they could think of; from the film *Shipyard Sally* they sang Gracie Fields' 'Wish Me Luck as You Wave Me Goodbye'. Everyone joined in and Bella didn't bother to wipe away the tears as they flowed freely down her cheeks. She'd miss her co-workers very much and hoped they'd all be safe and still around if they came to do a revue show in Liverpool in the not-too-distant future.

With still no word from Bobby, Bella resigned herself to the fact that he didn't want to know. She was sitting in the back room with her mam, waiting for the driver Basil was sending to collect her. He was picking up Fran and Edie too and taking them to a lodging house in Manchester. From there they would be rehearsing in a church hall with a military band in readiness for their first show.

Bella could feel her teeth chattering with nerves as she heard an engine stop outside the house. Mam ran down the hall and opened the door. Bella's small case was packed and standing in the hallway. She picked up her gas mask box, her handbag with her identity papers inside, and the bit of money she'd managed to save since she started working. Mam had written down the secretary's phone number for Olive Mount Hospital. It was only to be used for emergencies, but was handy to have, just in case.

Bella gave her mam a hug and Mam kissed her on the cheek. 'Now stay safe, be careful, and write to me as often as you get chance. But above all that, enjoy yourself as much as you can. Keep our lads entertained, especially the ones that are shipped home wounded. They deserve the best. Goodbye, my love.'

'Goodbye, Mam. And you stay safe too. I'll see you when I can.'

Mam's eyes were bright as she hugged Bella tightly. 'As that nice song goes, "I'll See You in My Dreams" and if you sing it please think of me. I love you, queen.'

'Oh, Mam, of course I will. And I love you too, please take care.' Bella wiped away her tears, picked up her case and went out to the waiting car, where the patient driver and a tearful Fran and Edie were waiting. She got in the back seat with them and rooted in her bag for a hanky. 'Oh, that was so hard. She looks lost standing on the step on her own.'

Fran nodded. 'So did mine. Oh I know she's got my gran, but she might as well as be on her own for all the sense she gets out of her these days.'

They waved to Bella's mam as the driver pulled away and headed for the main road and their destination of Manchester.

*

Basil was waiting for them at the lodging house in the Manchester suburb of Didsbury. He'd told them it was theatrical digs, and the landlady, Mrs Rosemary Burton, a tall woman with large upper arms and a pleasant smile, was used to acts of all kinds staying with her. She looked a no-nonsense type but friendly enough. Basil said she was a terrific cook and they wouldn't starve while they got to know the ropes. They'd be having a bit of a snack now and a cooked meal tonight after the rehearsals with a full band this afternoon.

Mrs Burton led them through to a dining room, where the tables were laid with cloths and one was set for them. 'Take a seat, ladies and Basil. I'll be back in a minute. Kettle's already boiled so you can have a nice brew while I make some sandwiches for you.'

She bustled away and Bella looked around. The house was large and standing in its own grounds. It had a grand but faded air and the huge windows with their stained-glass top panels, framed by gold velvet curtains, let in a lot of light. It made her think about Bobby's lovely home and she swallowed the lump that had risen in her throat.

She couldn't understand, after all the nice things he'd said to her, why he hadn't replied to her letters. It didn't feel right. But maybe he simply didn't want to tell her that it was over and he wanted to be with Alicia after all. It was a cowardly way of doing things and for now she must put him out of her mind and concentrate on being the best she could in her new career.

Chapter Fifteen

From her position onstage, Bella watched Basil's face as they performed with the five-piece band he'd assembled. His grin stretched from ear to ear and as each song ended he was up on his feet cheering and clapping. This rehearsal was one of the best they'd ever done, Bella thought. Working with the band was so different to working with just a pianist and the odd sax or trumpet player. They had a piano player, a drummer, a double bass player, a trumpet player and a saxophonist.

She smiled at Fran and Edie, who backed her lead vocals on the solo songs. Everything sounded fuller and this allowed all their voices to soar to capacity and blend in perfect harmony. The adrenaline surged through Bella's veins and she even tackled 'Over the Rainbow' as a solo without breaking down. She blocked out the thoughts of singing it with Bobby and instead let her mind carry a picture of Betty with a big smile on her little face. It added to the emotion she put into the song.

As the girls trooped offstage and joined Basil at a table, a lady brought over a tray of refreshments for them. 'That was fantastic, girls,' he said as they flopped down in their seats. 'We'll have another run-through tomorrow and then I feel we are ready to hit the troops. We'll be staying in Didsbury at Rosemary's while we do the north-west, Lancashire and Yorkshire. So at least we have a comfortable base for now and we'll find others on our way down south, or we'll stay in the camps if they've room for us. We'll have to play that by ear as we go. I hope that sounds like a good plan?'

They all nodded their agreement. 'Sounds good to me,' Fran said. 'I can't wait to get going.'

'Me too,' Bella and Edie chorused.

'We'll get you back to Rosemary's place now and then you can have a little rest before dinner tonight.'

'I'm going to get a shower,' Fran said. 'I've never used one before so that should be fun. We all live in tin-bath-in-front-of-the-fire homes,' she told Basil. 'Rosemary's home is luxury to us.'

Basil smiled. 'She's had many a star under her roof. George Formby, Arthur Askey, Gracie Fields, Wilson, Keppel and Betty, Max Miller, when they've done shows in Manchester theatres.'

The girls stared open-mouthed at him. Those were big names on the variety circuit and to think they'd be lodging in the same place they'd all stayed was amazing.

He laughed. 'Come on, you all look star-struck. Let's get you back to your rooms and you can ask Rosemary for her stories.'

*

Mary locked the front door behind her and set off down Victory Street to meet Ethel Hardy for work. A man was repairing the front window of number twenty-three and she stopped to talk to him. The house had been empty for over a year now, since the last tenants had moved away. It was a shame to let it go to rack and ruin. The window had been boarded up for a long time, since a lad had kicked a football through it months ago. She knew the man as John Barnes, an odd-job man who worked for the landlord who owned her own and most of the other houses on the street. 'Are we getting a new family in then?' she asked. 'Not before time.'

'A lady and her elderly mother, I believe,' he replied. 'She's been bombed out down near the docks. Her kiddies have been evacuated and her old fella's in France fighting. They put her up in a hostel but her mother is confused and they need a proper place to stay. The authorities pointed her our way. If you know of anyone that's got any spare bits and pieces to help her get set up again, I know she'd be dead grateful. She's lost everything.'

'Let me see what I can do, John. We all help each other out round here and I'm sure the neighbours will step up and give what they can. When's she moving in?'

'As soon as I've walloped some paint on the walls and fixed this window. Landlord's got a few decent carpet squares to fit that he's lifted from another place so it's better than bare floors. I'd say a week at the most, probably.'

'Right you are. If you give me a knock-on when it's about ready and I'll have a few things lined up for you to bring across. I'd better get off to work now, so I'll catch you tomorrow no doubt.'

'Aye, and thanks, Missus, that's really kind of you.'

Mary hurried away, thinking to herself about how she could help. The new neighbour could have the double bed from the girls' bedroom as it was pointless hanging on to it. Lord knew when Bella and Molly would be home, and they could maybe buy a couple of single beds for them when the war was over. They were a bit too grown up to be sharing now anyway.

John would have to come over, dismantle the bed and carry it downstairs and across the street, but he'd probably got a mate who could help him. That was a start and there was the bedding too and some curtains she'd replaced last year but one. Better than nothing at the windows.

Be nice to see number twenty-three with people in it again. Mary used to be friendly with the woman who had it before it was left empty. Sometimes the post had been delivered there by mistake. Hers was number twenty-eight. The postman was a bit short-sighted and occasionally got the three and the eight muddled up, but her neighbour had always popped over as soon as she'd realised the letter or bill wasn't for her. She waved at Ethel, who had come hurrying into view, and as they walked to the hospital Mary told her about the expected new neighbours and Ethel promised to root out a few bits and bobs.

*

The Bryant Sisters took a final bow and smiled and waved to loud cheers, whistling and shouts of 'More!' as they walked offstage to be replaced by Marvo the Magician and his partner, billed as The Glamorous Gloria on the concert poster. In the dressing room the girls changed out of their full-skirted dresses and into khaki uniforms ready to begin their Andrews Sisters act to open the second half of the show. Fran answered a knock at the door and let in Basil with a tray of cold drinks for them. The two-night show, at the Palace Theatre in Manchester city centre, for civilians as well as the armed forces billeted nearby, had so far been a great success.

'That was fabulous, girls,' he said. 'They loved you. Soon have you top of the bill. More cheers and clapping for you three than any of the other singing acts I've got on the books right now.'

Fran laughed and patted her red hair. 'Don't let Gloria hear you saying that.'

Basil shook his head. 'Those two need to retire. Glamorous and Gloria are not two words you'd put together these days. And Marvo is struggling with his bad back. Trouble is, there are not many youngsters around that are free to take over those types of variety acts now. The lads are all away fighting or stuck in camps here waiting to be sent abroad.'

'Where are we tomorrow night?' Bella asked, setting her uniform cap at a jaunty angle and smiling at herself in the mirror on the wall above a dressing table.

'We're setting off for the Midlands in the morning and then travelling on to Oxfordshire to play a couple of RAF camps. We'll spend Christmas down there.'

Bella frowned. 'Whereabouts in Oxfordshire are we playing? And if we're down there for Christmas does that mean we won't be able to spend it with our families?'

'I'm afraid so, love. It's too far to bring you back. And as for the camps, we'll be playing at RAF Benson and Brize Norton. All them lovely airmen need cheering up.'

Bella's stomach flipped. What the heck would her mam say if she didn't come home for Christmas? Maybe she could go and stay with the family that was looking after Molly, or perhaps she'd spend it with Fran and Edie's mam's. Once they were back at the digs tonight she'd write to Mam and let her know what was happening, and then she could make some plans so that she wasn't alone. But going to Brize Norton could mean bumping into Bobby, *if* he was still there, and that thought didn't fill her with the pleasure it should have done. There was still no word from him and she hadn't written to him since they'd left home. He hadn't even congratulated her on the success of the Bryant Sisters. Obviously got other things on his mind, now Alicia was in the area.

'Right, come on,' Basil said. 'Let's get the next half of the show on the road. Go and knock 'em dead, girls.'

Chapter Sixteen

Oxfordshire, December 1940

Bella stared up at the ENSA poster promoting their show that night at RAF Benson. The Bryant Sisters were now top of the bill. The poster was pinned to the wall of the large canteen run by the Navy, Army and Air Force Institutes, called the NAAFI by everyone, and at the top end of the large, seasonally decorated room a makeshift stage was in the throes of being constructed by several blue-uniformed airmen. She wondered if Bobby had seen a similar poster in Brize Norton and if so, did he realise that she was in Oxfordshire and would be singing in front of him on Tuesday night?

Or maybe he didn't even realise that the Bryant Sisters on the poster were actually the girls he'd sung with. If he hadn't received her letters then he would have no idea that they were now with ENSA and the name was officially theirs, and not just something they'd been accidentally named by George, or one they'd used at Speke Legion. The artistes would be spending Christmas billeted at Brize Norton and appearing on Christmas Eve in a special show in the NAAFI.

The last few weeks had been a whirlwind of shows in theatres and campsites and travelling the country while dodging air raids by dashing into nearby shelters wherever they were performing, sometimes still in their stage clothes. It certainly wasn't the glamorous lifestyle many of their fans seemed to think it was. But apart from that side of things, on the whole it was fun. They'd been backed by some fabulous bands from both the air force and army and a great camaraderie had been struck up with the troops, who begged them to come back again as soon as they could.

Bella felt sad as they left each camp, wondering who would still be around when they next visited. Many of the troops were being sent abroad and as fast as seriously injured servicemen were brought home, others were shipped away to take their place. It was heartbreaking to see so many with lost limbs, head injuries and even blinded, and all of them so young.

Fran still hadn't heard from Frankie and a recent letter she'd received from his mother told her that no one in the family had heard from him either, nor was there anything official to say he was missing, so no news was good news and until a telegram came telling them otherwise, they mustn't give up hope. Fran eagerly scanned the faces of all the soldiers they saw being brought in to see the shows in wheelchairs and even on stretchers, just in case Frankie had been sent to a different camp by mistake rather than the one he belonged to.

The girls' mams were spending Christmas Day together this year, at Fran's house with the elderly grandparents; and then Mam was going to her friend Ethel Hardy's for tea on Boxing Day, so at least she wouldn't be on her own, Bella thought. It was hard though, thinking about past times with her family, and little Betty, all excited that Father Christmas had been and the carrot she'd left for Rudolph had been eaten. Last year's disastrous Christmas Day she'd put to the back of her mind, along with Bobby's Boxing Day confessions of love that had amounted to nothing.

She still couldn't understand the reasons behind his non-response to her letters, especially when she'd written to him about ENSA. She thought he'd be absolutely thrilled for her and the others. It made no sense, but there was no point in dwelling on it. They had a show to perform tonight and she would give the performance of her life. The boys in the audience deserved nothing less.

In one of the makeshift dressing rooms Bella and the other girls took it in turns to use the only mirror to style their hair and do their make-up. Their new, full-skirted red dresses with sparkly bodices for the first half of the show, made by the seamstress who travelled with the ENSA team, were hanging on the back of the door along with white-fur-trimmed Alice bands for their hair. Basil said they'd look really Christmassy in red with a bit of white. They'd wear their usual military uniforms, which had just been dry-cleaned and pressed, for the second half as usual. They slipped into their dresses, zipping each other up and arranging their Alice bands on top of their heads, flicking out their hair onto their shoulders.

'Are you ready, ladies?' Basil shouted, banging on the door and making them jump.

Fran opened it and smiled. 'At your service,' she said with a laugh, giving him a salute.

'Wow!' Basil shook his head. 'You all look amazing. You'll knock 'em dead tonight. Just what these lads need to keep up morale. Open the show with a couple of favourites, the ventriloquist will follow you, he'll be followed by the dancing troupe and then the magician and you'll all finish that half with a couple of Christmas songs, as we discussed. I'm sure the lads will join in. The second spot will open with Jimmy Calvert and his comedy routine, more dancing from the troupe, then you girls performing your Andrews Sisters act in uniform, followed by a big finale with all of you.'

'Sounds good to me,' Bella said. 'And if that format goes well we can do the same in Brize Norton.'

'Got it in one,' Basil said with a smile. 'Right, I'll go onstage and do the warm-up, tell a joke or two and then bring you on. See you later.'

*

After finishing the first half with a rousing, jazzy version of 'Jingle Bells', the girls left the stage first, followed by the rest of the team, and made their way to the dressing room. Basil had sent in a tray of cold drinks and they sat down and enjoyed the fresh lemonade, emptying the jug between them.

'The air force band is really good, don't you think?' Bella said.

Fran nodded. 'One of the best we've sung with. Wish we could take them with us.'

'Especially that blond saxophonist,' Edie said, a dreamy look in her blue eyes. 'He's lovely.'

Fran and Bella smiled at each other. It wasn't often shy Edie showed much of an interest in a member of the opposite sex, but they'd noticed the young man in question looking at her and smiling a few times tonight from the moment the girls had walked onstage. Maybe after the show was over, and they all met up in the NAAFI for refreshments, he might come over and talk to her.

They got changed into their khaki uniforms and redid each other's hair, rolling the curls around their fingers and fastening them up with hairgrips so their hats would sit neatly in place. Sitting at the side of the stage, waiting for their turn, they laughed at Jimmy Calvert and his risqué jokes, many picked up from watching Max Miller no doubt, but he put his own spin on them.

'Don't know how he gets away with it.' Fran giggled. 'But he cheers me up, so that's not a bad thing.'

Jimmy left the stage and the dancing troupe ran on, amid cheers from the lads in the front seats as the girls began their high leg-kicking routine, never a step out of place in spite of the precariously high-heeled shoes they all wore.

'I'd break my neck if I wore heels that thin and high,' Edie said, shaking her head.

'You and me both,' Bella agreed, marvelling at how high those legs could go. 'That's it, they're taking their bow. We're up!' She jumped to her feet and smoothed down the skirt of her uniform.

'Ready, girls?' They waited until Basil announced them and then ran onstage to cheers and whistles.

Bella thanked the audience and asked if there were any requests for favourite Andrews Sisters songs. They came thick and fast but the most requested were 'Alexander's Ragtime Band', which was always a favourite, and 'Boogie Woogie Bugle Boy', which they saved until the end. The bugle player in the band blew out his notes to perfection. The uproarious applause as they finished followed the girls offstage.

The band played a couple of Glenn Miller instrumentals and then all the artistes came back on for the show finale, with the Bryant Sisters front of stage encouraging the audience to join in and sing along with 'The Twelve Days of Christmas'. Bella felt her spirits lifting higher than they'd ever been in the last twelve months as the troops stood up and cheered, clapped and waved as the performers filed offstage.

There'd been a lot to cope with: Betty's death, Bobby's declarations of love that amounted to nothing, Dad joining up, Molly moving to a safer place, and Mam, staying behind for now to hold the fort so they had a place to still call home. There were some things to be thankful for and this opportunity of performing onstage with her friends was more than Bella could ever have hoped for.

*

As the girls came offstage Edie turned as someone called her name. The blond sax player came dashing towards her. She told the others to go on ahead to the dressing room. She smiled at the young man, her stomach flip-flopping all over the place.

'Err,' he began. 'I just wanted to say how much I enjoyed that, working with you I mean, and I wondered if you'd join me later when we gather for a drink, after you've got changed.'

'I'd love to,' Edie said. 'Thank you.' She nodded her head towards the room they were using as a dressing room. 'I'll be about five minutes.'

He nodded. 'Okay, I'll see you back in the NAAFI.' He turned and dashed away, leaving Edie staring after him.

She should have asked his name. He obviously knew hers. She hurried into the room and whipped off her stage uniform, aware of two sets of eyes burning into her back. Fran and Bella were already changed into comfortable black slacks and blue sweaters, knitted by Fran's mam, their hair neatly brushed.

'Well?' Fran said. 'What did he want?'

Edie felt her cheeks warming and smiled. 'He asked me to join him for a drink.'

'And did you say yes?' Bella asked.

'I did actually.' Edie grinned. 'He also said he'd really enjoyed working with us. He seems very nice.'

Fran nodded. 'What's his name?'

Edie shook her head. 'I didn't ask, but he knows mine.'

Fran smiled. 'Well hurry up then, get dressed and we'll go and find out.'

Edie pulled on her slacks and a sweater in the same shade of blue as her friends, fluffed out her waves and straightened her fringe. She slicked her lips with pink lipstick and smiled at her mirrored reflection. 'Will I do?'

'You'll do fine,' Bella said, opening the door and leading the way.

In the NAAFI the band and the rest of the entertainers were seated around tables that had been set with a buffet and an array of bottles and glasses.

Basil called the girls over and they joined him at the table he'd reserved for them. The young blond saxophonist lifted his hand in a wave at Edie and asked if he could join them.

'Be our guest,' Basil said. 'I wish we could take you with us on our travels, Steven.'

'So do I,' Steven said, smiling at Edie. 'But I feel sure our paths will cross again – well I hope so anyway.'

*

As the old bus commissioned by ENSA to transport its entertainers rumbled towards Brize Norton camp on Christmas Eve, Bella's stomach felt like it was tying itself in knots. In fact the whole of her insides were churning and she hoped she wouldn't throw up. They stopped at the gates, engine running, and waited while Basil and the driver showed the on-duty guard their papers. Satisfied, the guard nodded, the large white gates opened and they were waved on through with another airman pointing the driver towards a group of huts that were separate from the rest of the camp.

'Here we go,' Fran said, nudging Bella's arm. 'You okay? You're white as a sheet.'

Bella nodded. 'Just feeling a bit nervous. I mean, what if Bobby's here?'

Fran frowned. 'Well, what if he is? He's got some explaining to do, hasn't he? You've done nothing wrong and all you are doing here is working officially, not chasing after him like some demented woman. Come on, you'll be fine. Let's hope they've got a decent NAAFI. I'm ready for a brew. It's ages since breakfast. Come on, dreamer,' she said to Edie, who was staring into space through the window. 'You can write to him,' she added as Edie turned her attention to Fran and blushed prettily.

'And I will,' she said as they got off the bus. The blond airman who had played saxophone with the band at RAF Benson had given her his details and asked her to drop him a line when she got time. His full title was Flight Lieutenant Steven Collins, but he'd told her to call him Stevie. Edie had promised to write when she got a chance. She'd also told him that their post was a bit hit and miss as sometimes it was sent on to them from a general collection point for ENSA members, only to miss them when they'd already left for another destination, so not to worry if she didn't reply right away to his letters.

Two smart young women dressed in the blue uniform of the WAAF greeted them individually as the entertainers assembled by the bus with their bags and suitcases. Bella's mouth dropped open as she recognised the slim-built blonde, with a bossy air about her, as Alicia. She frowned and nudged Fran. Now what the heck was Alicia doing here? When it came to Bella's turn the other girl, who was as dark as Alicia was blonde, shook her hand. Alicia was busy greeting Basil and looking full of self-importance. The young women led the entertainers to two large Nissan huts.

'One for the ladies and one for the gentlemen,' Alicia announced. As she turned in Bella's direction she paused and her mouth tightened momentarily into a thin line of disapproval.

Bella wondered if she'd been recognised. After all, she was in military uniform with her hair fastened up off her shoulders and her cap fixed firmly in place. But she'd recognised Alicia instantly in spite of *her* uniform and hair tucked under a cap. Alicia came to stand in front of her and frowned. 'It *is* Bella, I presume? I didn't realise you were in the forces. I thought you worked in the match factory.' This last was said with a tone of disdain in her voice and Fran rounded on her as Bella seemed lost for words.

'Yes, it is Bella,' she began. 'And no, we're not in the forces, we travel in uniform so that we look the part. We no longer work in the match factory. We are now part of ENSA and are known collectively as the Bryant Sisters. But then you'll know that already, won't you, Alicia? It will be on the poster you were sent and we're here to entertain your troops.'

Alicia's cheeks flushed pink and she spluttered over her reply. 'Oh, well, er well, yes. The name is on the poster in the NAAFI but I didn't connect it with Liverpool, not for one minute. I mean, why would I? I had nothing to do with that side of things back there.'

'What do you mean, that side of things?' Fran snapped.

'Well, the sort of things Robert got up to before we became engaged.' She raised her left hand and waggled her third finger, then put it down by her side again. 'Oh, I'm er, not allowed to wear my ring on duty.'

'You're engaged to Bobby?' Bella said; her voice was little more than a whisper.

Alicia nodded and turned away, a blush creeping up her neck as well as her cheeks now, but not before Bella had seen a look of panic in the girl's eyes.

The dark-haired girl showed them to their accommodation, which was clean and well set out with ready made-up camp beds. 'The showers are just in that little brick building next door, as is the toilet facilities. When you've unpacked, if you'd like to make your way over to the NAAFI, there'll be a nice cuppa and some sandwiches waiting for you.'

She was kind and the girls thanked her.

'I hope you'll be very comfortable and I look forward to the show later. I'm Marie, by the way. Alicia and I work in the administration department here on telephony and postal duties, as well as making sure our visitors are looked after and cared for. If there's anything you need, just give us a shout. There are clean towels in the shower room on the shelves. Just help yourselves. We'll see you later.'

Bella stared after the girl as she hurried away with Alicia, who had waited outside, on her heels. 'What do you make of that then?' she asked.

Fran shook her head. 'I don't know, but I'd want to scratch her eyes out if I were in your shoes. Engaged to Bobby indeed, is she? I'd like to know how that happened and why, after what he said to you. Makes him a bit fickle, doesn't it?'

Edie nodded. 'You've got to have it out with him if he's around, Bella. Something doesn't feel right.'

Bella sat down on the edge of her camp bed and burst into tears. Fran handed her a hanky. 'I smell a rat,' Fran began, narrowing her eyes. 'And didn't Marie say they both worked in the postal department? I wonder how long Alicia has been working there? I bet she's intercepted the letters you and he wrote.'

Bella blew her nose. 'Well it can't be that long, unless she started as soon as she and Bobby's mum moved down to Oxfordshire. But she wouldn't do that, surely? She'd get into really serious trouble if it were true.'

'She wouldn't if there was a witness to report her,' Edie said. 'But she's sly enough to make sure she was alone. We could ask Marie.'

'No, we can't go barging in and causing trouble like that,' Fran said. 'We'd be sent packing. We need proof first. You'll have to ask Bobby if he sent any letters to you after the first ones you received.'

Bella nodded. 'I will, if I see him. But Alicia and his mum didn't come down here until after I wrote to him and he didn't reply after the first few letters he sent, so the timing for that doesn't really fit, does it?'

'Hmm,' Fran said, wrinkling her nose. 'Well I still think there's something odd about it all and the fact that *she* said they're engaged now. I mean, crikey, he didn't waste much time. Anyway, let's go and get that cuppa. I'm spitting feathers here.'

Chapter Seventeen

Oxfordshire, Christmas Eve 1940

As the Bryant Sisters began their final song of the first spot Bella's eyes were fixed on the back wall of the NAAFI near the doors. The makeshift stage lights were bright in her eyes and it was difficult to make out anyone in particular, but as the doors had opened, and then closed quickly, she was almost sure she'd just seen Bobby slinking into the room. She blinked rapidly but was still blinded by the lights and it was almost impossible to make out any individual. Still, her stomach had turned over and her heart beat so hard she could feel it in her chest. She felt shaky and almost missed the opening chords. Fran gave her a nudge as the band struck up and she took a deep breath and concentrated on her singing.

The girls left the stage to uproarious applause and hurried into the dressing room. Bella leaned against the door and closed her eyes. They'd had a lovely day so far; afternoon rehearsals with a fabulous band made up of various members of the RAF and some of their own ENSA musicians, followed by a festive NAAFI meal that had left them so full to bursting that Fran had worried they'd never be able to do the zips up on their dresses.

It was hard to believe there was a war on and strict rationing with what they'd eaten today. All day she'd kept a lookout for Bobby, but apart from the quick glimpse of someone that she thought was him just now, there'd been no other sign. Alicia had been hanging around like a bad smell, mainly ignoring Bella and addressing Fran or Edie if she'd had to speak to the trio about anything.

Those stage lights had prevented her from seeing anything beyond the first few rows of airmen, so for all she knew he could have been sat at the back of the room and that man she'd seen wasn't him after all. Whatever, he must know by now that she was on the premises, surely; unless of course Alicia had decided not to tell him. Maybe neither of them was watching the show this evening. Perhaps they had left earlier and were spending Christmas with Bobby's mother at the place where she was staying.

Bella jumped as a knock at the door disturbed her thoughts. She opened it a fraction, and then wider as Marie smiled at her and handed her a tray of glasses and a jug of orange squash.

'That performance was so good,' Marie said, her round face beaming with excitement. 'They all loved it. We can't wait for you to come back on for more. Enjoy your refreshments.' She dashed away before Bella had a chance to say anything to her. She wanted to ask if Alicia was here tonight, which would probably mean that Bobby was too. She put the tray down and poured three glasses. Fran and Edie knocked theirs back in no time.

'I needed that,' Fran said, putting her glass back on the tray. 'Have you spotted him yet?' she asked Bella as she slipped her red dress off and placed it on the back of the door on a hanger.

Bella shrugged her shoulders. 'I'm not sure. I thought I saw a man that had a look of him coming in at the door but the lights were in my eyes so I couldn't really tell if it was him or not. He's probably not here. Might be at home with his mother and *her*.'

'I think Alicia is out there.' Edie nodded towards the door. 'I'm sure I saw her at the back of the room with a couple of lads in wheelchairs and she was showing some last-minute audience members to their seats, just before we started to sing.'

'Was she?' Fran asked. 'I didn't see her.' She shivered and pulled on her khaki uniform. 'It's cold in here. We could do with an electric fire or something to take the chill off.' She looked around the small room that appeared to be a storeroom, turned into a makeshift dressing room. There was a dark brown carpet on the floor with splashes of white paint on it, which was better than bare floorboards like some of the rooms they'd had to get changed in.

It's hardly Hollywood, Bella thought, smiling to herself. Her last letter from Mam, along with a Christmas card, had made her chuckle. Mam was telling everyone at work that her daughter was now in show business. She felt a small pang and half-wished she were at home with her, and then shook herself as she realised how lucky she was to be here where she felt relatively safe, not to mention well-fed.

Counting her blessings, she hurriedly got changed into her uniform. Edie pinned her hair up for her and she was just fixing her hat at a jaunty angle when another knock sounded at the door. A quieter knock this time, which wasn't Basil as he usually knocked loudly and shouted, 'Are you decent?'

Fran went to answer and stepped back with a shocked expression on her face. 'Edie,' she called. 'Come on; let's make ourselves scarce for a few minutes.' She bundled Edie out of the room as Bobby walked in and closed the door.

Bella's hand flew to her mouth and she stared at him, lost for words.

'How are you?' he asked, half-smiling, but the smile didn't quite reach his worried blue eyes.

'Okay, thank you. And you?'

He shrugged. 'It was a shock to see you out there onstage tonight. I saw the poster, but never for one minute did I think the act would be our own Bryant Sisters. I just assumed someone had taken the name for themselves. You could have at least warned me and let me know what was happening in your life.' His tone was bitter.

Bella frowned. 'But I *did* let you know. I wrote to you twice, even after you stopped writing to me. I told you we'd joined the ENSA team ages ago.'

'I never stopped writing to you,' Bobby said, shaking his head. 'I've written to you every single week and not had one reply, and certainly nothing to tell me about ENSA.' He ran his hands through his blond hair, which was shorter than he used to wear it. 'I assumed you'd met someone else and that was it. You didn't want to tell me things were over between us, so just stopped all contact.' He faltered and looked at her, his eyes anxious.

Bella took a deep breath. 'Bobby, I can assure you, I haven't had a letter from you for ages. I thought it was your way of breaking up with *me*. And when Alicia told me you were engaged, well it seemed I was right. You've chosen her above me after all.'

Bobby closed his eyes and gripped the back of a chair. 'When did you see Alicia?'

'Yesterday, when she and Marie met us off the bus as we arrived.'

He shook his head. 'I was out of the camp on business yesterday and didn't get back until this afternoon. She never mentioned that she'd seen you.'

Bella raised an ironical eyebrow. 'Well she wouldn't, would she? Not now she's got what she always wanted and she's your fiancée.'

He clapped a hand to his head and muttered, 'This wasn't meant to happen, Bella. I love you. Alicia pretty much forced my arm to get engaged after her father died last month. She knew I hadn't heard from you and said it was for the best and must have been meant to be as now she and I could be together.'

He stepped towards her and Bella stepped back, but he grabbed hold of her and pulled her into his arms, kissing her and holding her tight like he'd never let her go. 'I love you, Bella, I always will,' he whispered.

She could hear the emotion in his voice and felt tears running down her cheeks. She loved him, more than anything, even though he was no longer hers to love. 'But what about Alicia? You're engaged to her. It's too late, Bobby.' She wriggled out of his arms. 'You'd better go.' She swiped at her wet cheeks with the back of her hand.

'I'm going nowhere. We need to sort this mess out tonight. I've no idea why you didn't get my letters or I didn't get yours, but I will get to the bottom of it.'

'I'm back onstage soon,' she said. 'I need to compose myself, ready.'

He nodded. 'But I need to talk to you again later. I'll come and find you.'

'Okay. But Alicia will be looking for you.'

He shook his head. 'I'll wait until I know she's in bed. Are you in the visitors' Nissan huts?'

'Yes. It's the one closest to the shower block.'

He paused, his hand on the doorknob. 'Do you still sing "Over the Rainbow?"'

She smiled. 'Occasionally. And I am doing tonight, for Betty, for Christmas; in the finale.'

His face softened. 'I'll look forward to it. See you later.'

She closed the door behind him and took a deep shuddering breath as Fran and Edie burst in.

'What did he say?' Fran demanded. 'He looked white as a sheet and quite angry as he dashed past us in the corridor.'

Bella told them what Bobby had said.

'It's her, you can bet your life on it,' Fran said. 'She's been nicking the letters and hiding them, yours to him and his to you. There's no other explanation.'

Bella shrugged. 'Maybe. But that doesn't explain why I got a couple at first and then nothing for a few weeks *before* she joined the WAAF. Anyway, he's meeting me later to talk some more.'

'Good. Get it sorted out. Right, come on; let's give them all the best night of their lives.'

*

Bella peered through the smoky fug that filled the room before announcing the final song of the night. She could see neither Alicia nor Bobby as the pianist played the opening bars of her chosen song. Maybe they'd left already, she thought, although she could see Marie, right at the back of the room, smiling from ear to ear. So Alicia must be around somewhere; they usually worked as a pair.

She took a deep breath and, as an expectant silence filled the room, Bella began to sing 'Over the Rainbow'. Her eyes closed, her voice rang out clear and note-perfect. Picturing little Betty flying freely over the rainbow, she was conscious of a movement to her right and a hand slipping into hers as a familiar voice blended perfectly in harmony with her own. The emotion rose within her and carried her through to the final bars and she opened her eyes to see Bobby smiling into them.

The applause was thunderous and shouts of 'More!' and whistling and stamping from the air force audience had the Bryant Sisters and Bobby looking at each other with delight and grinning. Fran held up her hand and silence fell as she made an announcement. 'Just to let you know that Bobby here was one of our team back home in Liverpool and we performed together a lot. So it's a pleasure for us to have him back for a short time tonight, and we'll give you a couple more songs if you'll all join in.'

Bobby stood close to Bella as they all sang the final two songs, both popular Andrews Sisters choices. He linked his fingers through hers, hidden behind their backs, and she loved the warmth of him standing beside her, just like old times. Bobby singing with her again was the last thing she'd been expecting today, but it felt good. As they took a final bow and he whispered 'See you later' and jumped from the stage, she saw Alicia approach him with a furious look on her face. There seemed to be an angry exchange of words between them before Bobby took her arm and propelled her to the back of the room and out through the double doors.

'Oops, well that's well and truly put the cat among the pigeons,' Fran chuckled as they filed offstage. 'Alicia doesn't look too happy, does she?' She led the way into the girls' dressing room and flopped down onto a chair. 'I'm shattered. It's been a very long day. I'm looking forward to time off tomorrow and Christmas dinner here before we head off again.'

Bella shrugged as she changed out of her uniform and into her black wool slacks and a warm red sweater. They were travelling south on Boxing Day, avoiding London as it was deemed dangerous, and heading to Kent, near Basil's hometown, for New Year.

After that they would be back up north with a few days off that Bella planned to spend with her mam before they went back to the Didsbury digs. If Bobby wanted to resume writing to her, it would be a bit hit and miss but he could send the letters to her mam's house for now and she could send them on to Didsbury, where Bella would pick her post up when she could.

The girls grabbed a sandwich and a hot drink in the NAAFI and, rather than stay and socialise as they'd done at the Benson camp, took them back to their bedroom. They ate their supper and then, yawning, Fran and Edie got undressed for bed but Bella kept her clothes on, ready for when Bobby came to call.

'So what do you think he'll do?' Fran asked, climbing into bed and snuggling down under the extra blankets they'd been given.

'No idea,' Bella replied, running a brush through her hair that now fell in soft waves to her shoulders. She touched up her lippy and smacked her lips together. 'Will I do?'

'That's what I said last night.' Edie grinned. 'And of course you will,' she added as a soft knock sounded on the door. 'Here he is, slip your warm coat and your scarf on and good luck.'

Bella let Bobby take her hand as he hurried them away from the Nissan hut towards a wooden bench seat on the other side of the shower block. She shivered as they sat side by side. He put his arms around her and kissed her passionately and held her tight as though he'd never let her go. He kissed her again and she melted into him, realising just how much she'd missed him.

'I should have worn my big coat over my uniform,' he said breathlessly, as they broke apart. 'Then we could have slipped it over your shoulders.'

'I'm fine, really.' She didn't know if the shivering was from being in his arms again or from feeling cold. She smiled.

'Look,' he began. 'This engagement to Alicia, it means nothing and should never have happened. That sounds awful, I know, but the night after her father's wake, when we were with my parents, my mother said that what Alicia needed was stability and some hope for the future. It was her suggestion that as I was no longer involved with you, I was free to marry Alicia, just as they'd always hoped I would do.'

He sighed. 'Alicia jumped on that as a proposal and accepted. What was I supposed to do? I honestly thought you'd left me; with no letters coming from you what else was I to think? It's all such a mess. What should I do, Bella? Now I know you didn't let me down, I just want to be with you. I'm starting to have my suspicions as to why we didn't get each other's letters. Without proof I can't make accusations, but I think you know what I'm implying here.'

Bella nodded. 'Yes, I do, but you need to be careful. I was surprised to see her actually working here.'

'My father put in a good word as he thought it would be best for her to get some real-life experience and skills rather than hanging around with Mother and her friends all day.'

'She seems to enjoy her job.'

He shrugged. 'She says she does. And she's made some friends of a similar age, so that's something. I'm going to have to sit her down and tell her it's all been a mistake, the, er, engagement, I mean. Singing with you again tonight was just wonderful, it made my heart soar. I haven't felt as good as that for a long time, not since I left Liverpool. I really do love you, Bella, and I want to spend the rest of my life with you.'

A snapping noise, like someone standing on fallen twigs, and a nearby strangled cry stopped Bella from responding as Alicia, white-faced except for two angry red spots high on her cheeks, appeared in front of them.

'Oh, you do, do you?' she began in her high, piping voice. 'And what about me, Robert? You're supposed to be marrying me, or had you forgotten?'

Bella chewed her lip as Bobby leapt to his feet. 'Alicia, what do you think you're doing? Sneaking up like that and listening to a private conversation.'

Alicia folded her arms and glared at him. 'I saw you from the window of my billet, sneaking round here. I had a feeling you were meeting her,' she snapped, glaring at Bella. 'You haven't taken your eye off her all night.'

'Well you might as well as know,' Bobby began. 'Our engagement, for what it's worth, is off. Somehow or other Bella hasn't been receiving my letters, and for some strange reason I haven't been getting hers. We have no reason not to be together. It's what we want, what we always wanted.'

'Yes, well, there's a war on,' Alicia snapped. 'It's affecting everything, including the post.'

'Really?' Bobby raised an ironical eyebrow. 'Other airmen billeted here get post regularly. Makes you think.'

'Nothing to do with me.' Alicia shrugged. 'So what you are telling me is that our engagement is off? Is that right?'

He nodded and Bella frowned, surprised that the girl wasn't screaming at him as she'd seemed so angry at first.

Alicia let her arms fall to her sides, but she kept her head upright and stared at them both, a sly smile spreading across her face. She nodded slowly. 'Then it's a good job I've got your parents to look out for me, isn't it. Because when I tell them tomorrow over the Christmas Day lunch we're both supposed to be attending that I'm expecting their first grandchild, I hope *they* don't turn their backs on me like their son just did.'

And with that she flounced away, leaving Bobby staring after her with a look of horror on his face and his hand clamped to his mouth. He turned to stare at Bella, who was shaking her head.

'Did she just tell me she's pregnant?' he gasped.

Bella blew out her cheeks and nodded. 'I think so.' Suddenly she felt totally numb, like her heart had just fallen out of her chest.

'Shit! How the hell did that happen? We only, well you know, just once, a few weeks ago. It shouldn't have happened, it wasn't what I wanted,' he garbled, running his hands through his hair.

Bella raised an ironical eyebrow and got to her feet. She was too shocked to feel angry with him right now. 'Bobby. You'd better go after her. For some reason we're not meant to be. We can't. You'll have to do right by her. Your mother will go mad if you don't. I'm sorry.'

He grabbed her by the hand. 'It's me that's sorry. I can't believe this. I love you, so much.'

She nodded. 'And I love you too. But we can't do anything about it. I'm going back inside now.' She needed to get away before she begged him to stay when she knew that was impossible. 'Stay safe, Bobby. And good luck. It's been really nice to see you again.'

She walked away back to the Nissan hut and let herself in. Fran and Edie were flat out. She took off her clothes and hurried into bed, tears running freely down her cheeks. She cried herself to sleep, sobbing heartbrokenly into her pillow and feeling numb. From being on cloud nine and hoping once more that she might have a wonderful and happy future with Bobby, she now felt at rock bottom and back to square one.

Chapter Eighteen

Wavertree, May 1941

Mary smoothed the pink candlewick bedspread straight and looked around the room with pride. To give herself something to do on long nights when she was feeling fed up and lonely, she'd decided to decorate the second bedroom. After the old double bed had been dismantled and taken across the road to her new neighbour, Violet Perkins', house, she'd bought some brushes and repainted the walls herself in white distemper. It had taken hours but she was really pleased with how fresh the room looked now. She'd also picked up a pair of pink flowery curtains from Paddy's Market, which thankfully was still open, and shortened them to fit the window. And her friend Ethel Hardy had given her a nice single bed and the pink bedspread from her spare room.

Mary had been planning to wait until the war was over and Harry safely home before refurnishing the bedroom so that Molly and Bella could have new single beds instead of sharing the old double, but Bella was on her way home for a week's break before travelling to Scotland with the regular troupe of ENSA entertainers.

She hadn't seen her daughter since the beginning of the year when she'd had a couple of days break from touring, and the visit had been a bit of a gloomy one. Bella had seemed upset by the fact that Bobby Harrison was going to marry his parents' god-daughter, Alicia. Bella hadn't elaborated on the news. Just said she'd seen him at RAF Brize Norton on Christmas Eve and he'd sung onstage with the Bryant Sisters.

Mary had a feeling there was more to it than met the eye, but her daughter didn't want to talk or go into details so they'd left it at that and just enjoyed the time they had together. She was really looking forward to her visit and all being well Bella was being dropped off later this afternoon.

Mary hurried downstairs and put on her lightweight jacket. She picked up the shopping list she'd written and her purse and ration book from the table, slung her gas mask over her shoulder and her shopping bag over her arm and set off for the shops. There was that much to remember to take with you before nipping out these days, it was like planning for a day trip. Gone were the days when you could just pick up your purse and nip round the corner.

It was a pleasant day, bright sunshine and blue skies, which had put people in a good mood after a few days of drizzle last week. The queue at the butcher's shop was out the door and past the window. But there was no choice other than to wait or there'd be nothing for their tea tonight. She hoped the bakery had some cakes as it would be a nice treat. With everything like sugar and butter being scarce and not many fresh eggs around, Mrs Edwards, who owned the bakery, had a first-come-first-served policy on cakes. She did her best but once they'd gone, that was it until she had time to make more. There had been talk of adapting a bread recipe and creating a National Loaf to save money, which would be mainly brown flour as white flour was becoming harder to get. It didn't appeal to Mary, and some said it would be like eating cardboard, but if it happened it'd be better than no bread at all, she supposed.

By the time it was her turn at the butcher's counter she'd almost given up hope of getting any lamb to make a pan of scouse that would do them for two days, but as luck would have it there was a bit of neck fillet left on the tray and Jim the butcher cut it into chunky pieces for her.

'Anything else, Mary?' he asked, wrapping the lamb in grease-proof and popping it into a paper bag.

'A couple of bacon rashers please, and I don't suppose you've any eggs hiding under the counter? Our Bella's coming home later and it would be nice to give her a cooked breakfast in the morning.'

Jim winked at her and slipped two brown eggs into another bag and handed them over.

'That's my lot now. Hopefully the hens will have laid more by the time I close here today. I've a nice bit of cheese in this morning. Might as well as get your rations while I've got it. I can do you an ounce of Cheshire.'

Mary nodded. That was two meals each from the lamb, breakfast in the morning, and cheese on toast for dinnertime. They'd be dining like royalty at this rate. Although Bella had told her the troupe was well looked after at all the barracks they visited, which was good to know. She handed her ration book over and a ten-shilling note. There'd be enough change left to get her loaf of bread and a cake if possible. Mary pocketed her money and left the butcher's with a smile on her face.

In the bakery she was lucky enough to get a Victoria sponge cake and a white crusty loaf. She consulted her shopping list and hurried to the greengrocer's at the end of the road, praying they'd got the vegetables she needed. She'd already got an onion and some potatoes at home, so only needed carrots, and she liked to chop up a swede for her particular recipe if she could get one. And she was in luck again, as there were two swedes in the basket, along with a handful of carrots.

Mary hurried home, her mouth salivating at the thoughts of a decent pan of scouse. She'd hardly cooked at all for herself since she'd been on her own. She'd lost her appetite as well as weight, which was no bad thing as she'd piled it on when she was carrying little Betty and hadn't lost it all after her birth.

She felt fitter for the weight loss, but today she actually felt hungry for once. It would be good to sit down at the table with company rather than by herself. As she slotted the key into the lock a voice yoo-hooed from across the street and she turned to see her neighbour waving something at her. 'Oh, good morning, Violet. How are you, queen and how's your mam today?'

'Not so bad, Mary,' Violet said, hurrying across the street. 'Settling a lot better than I thought she would. She's not as confused as she was at first, now she's getting used to where everything is. Best thing ever, this house coming up for grabs.'

'It's nice to see it lived in again,' Mary said. 'Good to see nice fresh nets at the windows instead of a wooden board.'

'It was good of your mate Ethel to give me those. In fact, everyone has been so kind to us, I could cry. But I won't, because I'd rather give them a smile. Anyway, I've just been clearing some stuff that's been left outside in the back in sacks. There was some old post that John must have shoved in the sacks when he did the painting. But there's a couple of letters here that look like your surname's on them, except because they're damp it's hard to tell because the ink's all smudged. Your name is Rogers though, isn't it?'

'It is,' Mary replied. 'This happened a while ago when the other family lived there. The same postman mistook twenty-eight for twenty-three.' She took the letters and cards off Violet and stared at the names on the damp and dirty envelopes. She nodded; two had December postmarks on them so must be Christmas cards and the other two were letters addressed to Miss B. Rogers. She chewed her lip. It looked like Bobby's handwriting. The letters that Bella had never received had been lying in the empty house all along. Mary felt a wave of sadness rush over her. Poor Bella. Too late now though, if Bobby had already married that girl Alicia. 'Thanks very much, Vi.'

'You're welcome. I'll let you get on. See you soon.' Violet hurried back across the cobbles and into her own house.

Mary went indoors and dropped the letters on to the table while she put her shopping away. She made a pot of tea and poured herself a mug. Sitting at the table, she picked up one of Bobby's letters and looked at the Oxfordshire postmark. The date just about fitted in to the time Bella had stopped hearing from him. Well as her own mam used to say, 'what will be, will be,' she thought. There's a reason for everything and maybe Bella and Bobby weren't meant to be together. Mary was a firm believer in what fate had in store for everyone, and maybe Bella hadn't met her true love match yet.

*

'See you tomorrow,' Bella called as the car carrying Fran and Edie drove away up Victory Street. She knocked on the front door and smiled as her mam yanked it open, beaming. Bella flung her arms around Mam and hugged her tight, tears running down her cheeks and mingling with her mam's. 'Oh it's so good to see you, Mam,' she cried as she was pulled inside and down the hall to the back sitting room. 'I've really missed you.'

'Not as much as I've missed you, love,' Mam said, wiping her eyes on a hanky she took from her cardigan pocket. 'Sit down and I'll make you a nice cuppa.'

'Something smells good,' Bella said, sniffing the air with appreciation.

'Lamb scouse. For our tea. Thought we'd push the boat out seeing as I've had no one to cook for lately. I intend to spoil you while you're home.'

Bella sat back in her dad's armchair and stretched out her legs. She looked around the spotlessly clean room that held so many family memories for her. It was so tidy. Too tidy. No books or jigsaw puzzles or dollies and boxes of bricks lying around, or copies of the *Liverpool Echo* stashed under the chair. It was as though the family she'd lived with was no more and it made her heart ache. God only knew how her mam must feel, night after night, sitting here all alone.

'Bella.' Mam's voice broke her thoughts and she looked up and smiled. Mam rooted in her pocket and pulled out some envelopes. She handed them to Bella. 'These had been posted through the empty house letterbox, chuck. Lord knows how long ago. The postmarks are a bit smudged but they're from Oxfordshire, so no doubt written by Bobby. I wanted you to have them straight away.'

Bella felt her jaw drop. Bobby's letters. So like he'd told her, he had written after all. But how come she'd got the first few and not these?

'That older postman's been back in our delivery area so he probably got the numbers mixed up again,' Mam said, as though reading her mind. 'He's needed new glasses for years. It used to happen a lot, our post going over the road, and then they took him off this round and put a younger fellow on, but of course he'll have joined up. We've been back to the old fellow for a while now.'

Bella sighed and her eyes filled. Alicia must have stolen the final few, and the letters Bella had sent to Bobby. There was no other explanation. *What a mess.* But it was too late now, anyway. He'd be married to the girl and their baby wouldn't be long before it arrived. She couldn't even write to him to tell him she'd now got his missing letters in her possession. What was the point? If Alicia was still working she'd just do as she'd done before and steal them. Bobby was lost to her forever and it was time to move on. She knew she had plenty of admirers, but her heart wasn't into getting involved with anyone at the moment. She slipped the letters into her handbag at the side of her chair. She couldn't bear to read them today; maybe later in the week when she felt stronger.

'Are you not going to look at them, chuck?' Mam asked, her head on one side.

Bella half-smiled and shook her head. 'Maybe later.'

Mam nodded. 'Right, well I'll get you that cuppa and then we'll have a bite to eat.'

'Is there anything you'd like to do this afternoon, love?' Mary asked, clearing the plates and mugs from the table after their dinnertime cheese on toast.

'Actually, Mam, yes there is. Can we get the tram into the city? I've promised to look for some Pan Stik foundation as we're running out, and some nice red lippy and nail varnish. It's not always easy to go shopping when we're travelling up and down the country as the driver likes to stick to the main roads and most shops are in town centres and he always has a grumble if he has to break the journey. And a lot of places have been bombed and shops are closed. We could get a nice cup of coffee at the Kardomah.'

Mary nodded. 'That'll be nice, love. We haven't been shopping for a long time. You can look in Lewis's for the make-up. Pan Stik's Max Factor make, isn't it?'

'It is. And they've got a counter in Lewis's. I'll just pop to the carsey and then nip upstairs and get ready. This will be funny. I've not been to a real outside toilet since leaving home. Most of the camps have them in shower blocks.'

'Well at least it's a nice day and it won't be frozen,' Mary said. 'How's Ken next door coping with the air raids you've had?'

'He's not here, chuck. He's at his sister Minnie's on the Wirral. They came for him a few weeks ago just before Minnie's boys went away. He's keeping her company – or winding her up more like.'

Bella laughed.

'But anyway, the house is shut up. I keep my eye on it and Flo next to him's gone to her brother's in Chester. I'm pretty much on my own in this row at the moment. I don't like it, but there's not a lot I can do about it.'

*

Bella hurried up the yard to the toilet block, feeling worried. The thoughts of her mam on her own at night in that cellar when the air raid sirens went off really bothered her. Tonight she would have a good talk with her and try to persuade her to join the family Molly was staying with in Wales.

She could shut the house up and as long as the rent was paid each week, so they all had a home to come back to, it would save Mam money. There'd be no bills to pay as no one would be using gas and electricity, so the meters wouldn't need feeding their regular shilling pieces. She'd save on food shopping too; in the country there was no real shortage of fresh food like there was here. Mam would have company and be a lot safer.

As they hurried to get the tram, Bella linked her arm through her mam's. On the journey into the city, the evidence of destruction appalled her. 'I can't believe how bad it is round here,' she said as they neared the Dock Road.

Mam nodded. 'Well, you hear about the damage on the wireless and see it in the *Echo*, but until you witness it with your own eyes, it doesn't hit home. I'd no idea it was this bad, although Violet said a lot of the tenements near where she came from had been flattened and many streets of terraces are gone as well as schools and churches. It's shocking. There'll be nothing left at this rate. Good job we've come down today while we still can.'

'I'll get my shopping first before we go and get a brew,' Bella said as they made their way to the junction of Renshaw Street and Ranelagh Street where Lewis's store entrance stood. At the Max Factor counter she chose her red lipstick and matching nail varnish and asked for a Pan Stik in a natural colour.

'Last one,' the girl on the counter said, dropping her purchases into a paper bag. 'That was lucky.'

Bella smiled. 'It was indeed.'

They had a wander around the sales floors looking at clothes. 'Not got much choice,' Mam said as they admired a rail of summer dresses. 'Nothing like they usually have. And it was on the news the other night that from next month we're all getting clothing coupons and will only be allowed to buy so much. I think it's because all the clothing factories are making uniforms for the troops and nurses. There's not a lot of ordinary clothing being made. I wish I could sew. I'd make meself a nice dress. I love knitting but could never master needlework at school.'

'Me neither,' Bella said, smiling. 'You used to alter our clothes though when we were little.'

'Oh I can turn up hems and put collars and cuffs on things, but I get them ready made or unpicked from things I buy cheap at Paddy's Market, and they just need a few stitches to hold them in place. Well, there's not much here. Shall we have a quick look in Blacklers before we go to the Kardomah?'

'We've got a nice lady that comes along with us on the ENSA bus does all our sewing,' Bella said as they left the store. 'She makes lovely dresses and there's always someone's outfit that needs repairing and buttons replacing. I hope we can still get materiel for dresses for our shows or we're going to be stuck. We've a few nice things but we'll need more as the year goes on.'

Mam nodded. 'Well, all being well this war will be over by Christmas. That's what people are saying anyway. All I want is to get back to normal and have my family home with me again.'

Bella puffed out her cheeks. 'Let's hope so, Mam.'

In Blacklers Bella managed to get a pair of stockings, and treated her mam to some warm blue slippers with thick rubber soles. She'd noticed earlier that her old ones were all broken down at the back, and that was dangerous if she had to get down to the cellar in a hurry. She'd end up breaking her neck if she fell down those stairs, and no one would be any the wiser until it was too late.

As they sat in the Kardomah drinking coffee and looking out over Bold Street Bella stared at a woman and a slim, blonde girl on the other side of the road, carrying large bags of shopping. They momentarily disappeared from sight behind a bus.

Mam saw Bella looking and followed her gaze, but the women were getting into a car now that blocked her view. 'Do you know them women, chuck?'

'Well I didn't get a proper look, but I thought it was Bobby's mother and Alicia,' Bella said, frowning. 'But it can't be. They're supposed to be in Oxfordshire, or at least I thought they were. And, er, well Alicia looked far too slim to be in the family way,' she finished, looking down at her cup of coffee.

Mam gasped and put her hand to her mouth. 'You never told me she was expecting.'

Bella sighed. 'That's the reason they were getting married, Mam. She told Bobby she was pregnant after he sang with me at one of our shows. He wanted us to be together. We'd talked about neither of us getting each other's letters and he said he'd tell her it was over between them, but she was hiding nearby and overheard our conversation and just blurted it out.'

'Oh, Bella,' said Mam. 'I'm so sorry, love.'

'I told him to go after her and that we couldn't be together if she was, and that was it. She'd been working on telephony and postal duties for the WAAF at Brize Norton for a while and Bobby suspected she'd been hiding our letters to each other, although he didn't really have any proof of that but it seems the only logical explanation. Well apart from the t-two letters you gave me that ended up across the road...' Her voice finally cracked.

Mam pursed her lips. 'Well it sounds about right that she would do that. The devious little madam. So this baby would be due about when?'

Bella shrugged. 'I don't know exactly, but that was Christmas Eve she told him. Bobby looked really shocked. He hadn't been expecting her news. She said she was planning on telling all the family on Christmas Day. She didn't have any signs of a bump so she must have been only a few weeks gone then.'

Mam counted on her fingers. 'So it's May now, that's five months this year just, and one or two at the most from before Christmas would make her six or seven months and she's slim as a rake and running around Liverpool shopping today. That doesn't add up. Do you think she was lying to trap Bobby?'

'That's what Fran and Edie said.'

'Well there's only one way to find out. We'll call round to see them on the way back. Say we spotted them in the centre and realised they were back home from Oxfordshire.'

'Oh, Mam, we can't do that,' Bella protested.

'We can. Well I can, anyway. Just to see how they are, being neighbourly, like. You can go home or to Fran's, and I'll nip round to Fenella's place. I'll get to the bottom of things, don't you worry. If that young madam has lied it'll show all over her face. I'll tell them you're home for a few days and watch how she takes it. She will know you've told me what happened. I'll call her bluff.'

Bella shook her head and took a sip of her coffee, which was now cold. She pushed the mug away and sighed. 'But, Mam, Bobby's married to her now, so what difference will it make?'

Chapter Nineteen

After leaving Bella and their shopping back at the house, Mary hurried across The Mystery Park and knocked loudly on the Harrisons' front door, which was opened by Margaret in her neat uniform.

'Afternoon, Margaret. I was just wondering if Mrs Harrison was home today.'

'Oh, is it Mrs Rogers?' Margaret peered short-sightedly at Mary, who nodded her head.

'It is,' she replied.

'Come in, please. I'll just let Mrs Harrison know you are here. I take it she isn't expecting you. She didn't tell me we were having guests today.'

'No, she isn't expecting me. I've just called on chance. I think I spotted her in the city earlier but she'd gone before I realised it was her.'

'Ah yes. She and Alicia have been shopping. If you'll just wait a moment.' Margaret hurried off down the hallway to the last door on the left and tapped before entering.

Mary heard the murmur of voices and then Margaret was back. 'Follow me, please.'

Mary followed her to the drawing room. 'Mrs Rogers, madam,' Margaret announced, before leaving the room.

'Mary, dear, how very nice to see you,' Fenella said. 'Please, take a seat.' She gestured to the sofa near the window and Mary sat down. 'To what do I owe the pleasure?'

'Eh?' Mary said, confused. *Why the devil doesn't she say what she means?*

'How are you, dear? Would you like a cup of tea?'

Mary nodded. They were on safe ground now. 'Yes please, I would that.'

Fenella picked up a little brass bell from a nearby table and shook it a few times.

Margaret popped back into the room. 'Yes, madam.'

'Tea for two please, Margaret. And have we any of Cook's lovely scones left?'

'I think so. I'll see what I can do.' Margaret smiled and left the room again.

'Are you home for good?' Mary asked. There was no sign of the girl, Alicia.

'Just for a few days,' Fenella replied. 'We had some legal business to attend to locally for Alicia's father's estate. So we thought we'd come back here until we venture back to Oxfordshire after the weekend. We managed to do some shopping, but I must say the city has taken some bad hits since we went away. Although it's not quite as bad as London. It's far too dangerous to venture down there at the moment. How are your family coping, Mary?'

'As best they can. Molly is evacuated to North Wales and she seems happy enough. My husband Harry is somewhere abroad, but Lord knows where. And Bella is travelling around with ENSA, doing her bit, singing for the troops. They say she's the next Vera Lynn, you know. I'm that proud of her.'

Mrs Harrison raised an eyebrow. 'Yes, I heard she's doing very well with ENSA now. Robert mentioned it last Christmas.'

'Did he? He sang along with the girls at the show,' Mary said. 'They enjoyed it, and so did he.'

Fenella's lips formed a straight line. 'Yes, well he won't be doing that any more. He's learning to fly now and will be too busy to be messing around. Also, he has his dear wife Alicia to consider these days.'

'Ah, so he did get married then?' Mary said as the door opened and Margaret pushed a laden tea trolley into the room.

'Indeed he did. Just after the New Year. Alicia is having a lie-down. She's not too well at the moment.'

Mary nodded as Fenella poured tea into two dainty china cups.

'Help yourself to sugar,' she invited and handed Mary a tea plate with a buttered scone.

'I hope it's nothing serious,' Mary said. 'Alicia, I mean. Only I heard from Bella that a baby was due soon. Hope all is well in that respect.' She watched closely as Fenella took a deep breath as though considering her answer before replying.

'Alicia lost the, er, baby, shortly after the wedding. It's taking her a while to get over the shock.'

'I'm very sorry to hear that,' Mary said, but she doubted there'd ever been a baby anyway. It had been a ploy by Alicia to get her claws into Bobby and stop him being with Bella. The poor lad. And as Mary's thoughts turned murderous the door flew open and Alicia bounced into the room, wearing a light-coloured dress suitable for dancing in.

'Aunty Fen, it fits like a dream and it feels lovely on. It's just right for the next officers' dance at the camp.' She stopped in her tracks and stared at Mary, her cheeks turning bright pink as she realised she and Fenella weren't alone. 'Oh, sorry. I didn't realise you had a visitor.'

Fenella introduced them. 'This is Mary Rogers, Bella's mother, and this is my daughter-in-law, Alicia,' she said. 'You seem to be feeling much better, my dear.'

'I am, thank you. Nice to meet you, Mrs Rogers,' Alicia said, with a smile that didn't reach her eyes. 'I hope Bella is well.'

Mary nodded. 'She is, thank you. She's just on a short break before travelling up to Scotland to work. The ENSA team are very busy keeping the troops' morale up.'

'Yes, er, we did meet briefly at Brize Norton.'

'So I believe,' Mary said, watching the girl flush a deep red. 'Bella said you were working there. Postal duties, wasn't it?'

'And telephony,' Alicia replied.

'I expect you'll be going back to work there when you return to Oxfordshire. We all have to do our bit, don't we?' Mary's voice was laden with sarcasm. These two wouldn't know an honest day's work if it slapped them around the face.

'Oh, Alicia won't be returning to work now she's a married woman,' Fenella answered for her.

Mary laughed. 'But we're all married women. The ladies that work in the factories, on munitions etcetera, are, in the main, married women. Like I say, we all have to do our bit and keep the country running while our men are away fighting for us.'

Fenella looked at her watch. 'Well, that's as maybe,' she said. 'But some of us do our bit in other ways. We are due to go out shortly, Mary. Don't think me rude in hurrying you along. It was very kind of you to think about us.' She stood up as Mary put the last bit of scone in her mouth and took another sip of tea.

Alicia excused herself and dashed out of the room. Mary raised an eyebrow. 'Made a good quick recovery since you said she wasn't well earlier.' She finished her tea, taking a deliberate amount of time, as she suspected they weren't in a hurry to go anywhere and just wanted rid of her. Finally she put down her cup and got to her feet. Feeling the devil sitting on her shoulders, she couldn't resist asking, 'Do you ever see anyone from our old schooldays, Fenella?'

'Old school? I'm not sure what you mean, Mary,' Fenella replied quietly.

'Old Swan Primary School, do you ever see any of our old mates?' Without waiting for a reply, she walked to the door and into the hall. 'I'll see meself out,' she announced as Fenella hurried after her, her face as white as the paintwork around the doorframe.

'That's a time in my life I don't wish to speak about,' Fenella hissed as Mary opened the door.

Mary smiled. 'Your secret's safe with me. But that one up there,' she raised her eyes to the ceiling, 'that little madam has got you wrapped around her little finger and I think you know it. She's not the one for your boy, but too late now, she's trapped him. I'll swear to God there was no baby. She's a liar.'

And with that she walked away, leaving Fenella standing on the top step, clinging to the door with her mouth opening and closing like a fish out of water. Mary took a deep breath and felt pleased with herself. That little showdown was for Bella. Fenella didn't call after her to put her right, so she'd bet her life she'd hit the nail on the head. Sadly it was too late now for her daughter and Bobby, but she felt a whole lot better for having her say.

*

As the air raid siren woke her from a deep sleep that night, Bella turned over and wondered for a moment where she was. Then, remembering she was at home on Victory Street, she jumped out of bed and pushed her feet into her slippers, grabbed her handbag and gas mask box and hurried onto the landing. Mam was making her way out of her bedroom at the same time, wearing her new slippers.

They dashed down to the cellar and climbed into their camp beds as engines droned overhead, so low Bella swore she felt the house shaking with the vibration. She hoped they wouldn't take the slates off the roof. Loud rumblings sounded in the distance as bombs exploded, probably on the docks and nearby streets where not a lot was left standing. Bella chewed her lip. *When will it all end?* It seemed to be getting worse, not better.

Almost every night for the next seven days Liverpool suffered its worst bombardment. The areas of Bootle and Birkenhead were badly damaged and when Bella saw the pictures in the *Echo* of the state of Lewis's and Blacklers' stores she couldn't believe her eyes.

They'd only been standing in those shops a few days ago. A cargo ship had been blown up on the docks, making even worse the already short supply of goods.

After Mam had gone to work, Bella got a pad and pen out of the sideboard drawer and wrote to Molly, telling her that she was putting their mam on the train to join her. Molly would get this letter tomorrow, in time to let her evacuee family know, and they could arrange to meet Mam at Llandudno station and take her out to the farm to stay. Bella was going to insist that her mam tell her boss at Olive Mount tomorrow that she was finishing and it would be her last day.

There was no way she could leave her here, alone, in this house. She'd never be able to concentrate on her singing or anything. It was time to put her foot down and make Mam realise that to survive this war she needed to be out of Liverpool. It was bad enough not knowing where Dad was, but at least Mam and Molly would be safe and that was one less thing to worry about. She finished her letter, addressed an envelope and set off for the post office. With a bit of luck the letter would go off with the dinnertime collection.

Standing in the queue, Bella listened to the conversations going on around her. People were talking about the terrible mess their city was in. One lady was saying that her next-door neighbour had lost her son the other day and was inconsolable. She wondered if Fran had heard anything yet about Frankie. She'd seen little of Fran and Edie since they'd arrived home, as both wanted to spend as much time with their mothers while they could. She paid for a stamp and put her letter in the pillar box on the street, then set off for Fran's house.

'Come on in, chuck,' Fran's mam said as she opened the door. 'She's in the back room with Edie. I'm just dashing to the butcher's while they keep an eye on Gran for me.'

Edie and Fran were sitting at the table hugging mugs of tea. Fran looked up and smiled wearily, big dark shadows beneath her eyes. 'Morning, Bella. You look as bad as I feel. Awful night again, wasn't it?' She picked up a sheet of paper and waved it in the air. 'But at last I've heard from Frankie. He can't say where he is or anything, but at least he's alive and not captured as we all feared he might be.'

'Oh thank God for that. What a relief for you.' Bella gave Fran a hug and Edie joined in. 'It's horrible right now. I can't believe how bad it is here in Liverpool. When we're away, we seem isolated somehow. Oh I know we see bombed-out buildings and churches and stuff, but it's more concentrated in Liverpool. I've just posted a letter to our Molly telling her to expect Mam any day soon. Mam doesn't know yet that she's going, but she is. I'm not taking no for an answer either.'

'I don't blame you,' Fran said, lifting the teapot and pouring a mug for Bella. Help yourself to milk, but you can only have half a spoon of sugar. We've not got much left. Mam's trying to get a bit while she's shopping.'

'Thanks.' Bella took a welcome sip of her tea. 'I've got something to tell you.' She told them about her mam's visit to Bobby's home and how Mam was sure that Alicia was lying all along, but that she was now married to Bobby.

'Well, me and Edie said that all along,' Fran said and Edie nodded.

'Poor Bobby,' Edie said. 'Why don't you write to him while Alicia's out of the way?'

'Oh I couldn't do that. Marie might tell her that Bobby got a letter from someone and she'd demand to know who from and it might cause trouble for him. No, I have to get over him and move on with my life. There'll be plenty of time to meet someone new in the next few years. For now my singing comes first.'

Chapter Twenty

Basil rounded his troupe up for rehearsals for their Christmas Eve show at RAF Burtonwood. It was a new airbase and the facilities were better than many they'd used before, with nice shower and toilet blocks, which had pleased his girls. There was talk of the place also becoming a base for the USAAF – United States Army and Air Force – soon, as rumours were flying in all directions that the Americans were coming to the UK to assist with the war effort.

The attack by the Japanese on Pearl Harbor earlier this month had resulted in much damage to ships and over 2,400 people were reported to have died. A few days later, Hitler's declaration of war on the USA had led the United States to enter the war in Europe. It wouldn't be too long now before the country was awash with American soldiers and airmen.

The band the Bryant Sisters were currently singing with was made up of English musicians and two Americans, including the leader Earl, who had arrived early, ahead of the expected schedule of troops. Earl Franklin Junior had introduced himself to them all that morning and Basil had seen Bella's face light up for the first time in ages. She seemed drawn by the way his big dark-brown eyes constantly twinkled in her direction.

'He can't take his eyes off you,' Basil had heard Fran mutter in between songs. 'And he's very handsome. Look at those cheekbones. Cor.'

Basil smiled as Bella nodded her agreement. He also had to agree. Earl was indeed handsome, tall and slim, with finely chiselled features, including his high cheekbones and thick black hair that sat in a tidy air-force-style short back and sides. He was a great band leader, singer and swing-style piano player. He also played a trumpet well. He cut a fine figure onstage and his movements when he sang and played encouraged everyone to join in with him.

Basil sat watching them through a cloud of cigar smoke, nodding his head from time to time. Earl was very good. He'd told Basil that he came from New Orleans; the same place as one of Basil's favourites, Louis Armstrong, although Earl's voice was more melodic, deep, but not as gravelly as Louis's. When he sang with Bella the hairs on the back of Basil's neck stood on end. It was pure perfection. If only there wasn't a bloody war on, those two could go far. Their voices blended in perfect harmony and they looked great together. They were exactly the duo he'd been searching all his life for; they had star quality.

The singers took a break while the rest of the acts practised their performances for later. The girls joined Basil, and a lady in uniform brought over a tray of coffee and cakes. Basil beckoned for Earl to join them and he sauntered over and took the empty seat next to Bella. He smiled and winked at her and Bella blushed deeply but smiled back.

Fran nudged Basil and he nudged her back. He also nudged Edie on his other side and she smiled at him. They were all on the same wavelength, thinking the same, Basil thought. Bella was showing signs of coming back to life after her disappointment over Bobby. It was good for her to have a new male voice to blend with. With a bit of luck they might be able to take Earl and his band with them from time to time until the rest of his air force troop arrived and he was needed to fly planes, for Earl was a wing commander whose flying services would soon be required.

'Right, give me one more song and then you can go and rest before tonight's show,' Basil said. 'Seeing as it's a cold day, and will no doubt be a cold night, what about "I've Got My Love to Keep Me Warm", not many do that and the film it's from was really popular back in the late thirties, it'll be a good song to make your own. Here.' He rooted in his bag and pulled out the sheet music. 'Just in case you don't know it.'

'Oh, I do,' Earl said, smiling. 'Nice song for a cold winter's night.' He looked at Bella, 'Do you know it, Bella? Written by Irving Berlin.'

She nodded. 'I do. I remember seeing *On the Avenue* at the pictures with Mam when I was quite young.'

'Come on then,' Earl said, grabbing her hand and pulling her to her feet. She snatched her hand away and he raised an eyebrow. 'Sorry, ma'am,' he apologised. 'No offence meant.'

'None taken,' Bella said. 'I'm sorry too. It was just a shock, that's all.'

'But a beautiful girl like you must have her hand held several times a day, surely?' Earl teased.

'Not any more,' Bella muttered, looking down at the floor.

'Let's get on with the song,' Basil said. He could see how flustered Bella was and didn't want Earl to think it was because of his race that Bella had snatched her hand away. People could be prejudiced, but he didn't think Bella was that sort of person. He'd explain to Earl later that she'd been hurt and wasn't as trusting as she used to be. Earl seemed a nice guy and Basil was sure he'd understand Bella's reticence once he knew the reason behind it.

On the stage again, Bella and Earl, with Fran and Edie doing the backing vocals, made a good job of the song. Earl played trumpet as well as singing. Basil and the rest of the troupe clapped and cheered as the song finished and Bella and the others took a bow.

'Fabulous,' Basil declared. 'Save it for your party piece at the end of the show.'

*

Back in the Nissan hut they'd been given for a couple of nights, the girls lay down on the comfortable camp beds to rest.

'I could sleep for a week, never mind perform tonight,' Bella said. It had been quite an emotional day. She'd been able to speak to her mam and Molly this morning at the farmhouse they were staying in, and although the line had been crackly and a bit distorted it was good to hear their voices again. Mam told her she'd had a recent letter from Dad and he sent his love to them all. It was a relief to know he was all right. She missed them all so much and would give her right arm to be with them tomorrow.

Instead, she would spend it here with Fran and Edie; they'd have their Christmas dinner in the NAAFI, and a there was a buffet and dance on Christmas night that the ENSA variety troupe had been invited to join in with. She knew how lucky she was when others would be going hungry and had no one to spend their Christmas with. For so many families it would be their first Christmas without their lost loved ones, a time of great sorrow instead of the joy that a family Christmas should bring.

'Me too,' Fran said, yawning. 'Sleep for a week, I mean. But we'll be fine once we're all dolled up and the adrenaline starts flowing. A small glass of sherry wouldn't go amiss either. Fingers crossed we get offered one.'

'I think you and Earl sang so well together,' Edie said to Bella. 'Easily as good as you and Bobby used to.'

Bella felt her eyes beginning to fill. She'd been trying not to think about Bobby, but it was the time of year that reminded her of him the most. 'It's a year ago tonight since I last sang with Bobby. Even though I try not to, I often think about him and how the er, marriage is working out. Mam reckoned there was no baby, so I hope things are okay between them. It seems so cruel, what Alicia did to him. Me and him could have been engaged now, or even married.'

Fran nodded. 'But we don't know for certain that there definitely was no baby. That's just your mam's own thoughts and opinion. If there was, and Alicia genuinely miscarried, then you've got to feel a bit sorry for her and for Bobby, of course. Anyway, whatever the truth, Bobby's married to her now and you have to let go and see what the future brings.'

'Earl's really nice and seems quite taken with you, Bella,' Edie said, twiddling a curl around her fingers. 'He's got a lovely way about him. Makes me smile.'

Bella sighed. 'He is a bit of a charmer. But he's going to be really busy when the rest of the troops arrive and he'll be off flying planes and lord knows what else they'll be doing. This isn't the right time to get involved with anyone new. None of us know what the next few months will bring, or if we'll even survive them.'

'Bloody hell!' Fran exclaimed. 'Right Job's comforter you are, Bella. Of course we'll survive. We have to. We've got thousands more troops to entertain over the next year or two. And we've got Frankie and Stevie to keep cheerful for. They don't want to receive letters from home full of doom and gloom. They've got enough of that as it is. Come on, put on your happy face again and let's get ready for the show. We're getting too maudlin lying around in here.'

By the time the final part of the show got underway, Bella felt on top form. That adrenaline stuff that Fran was always going on about was a right good pick-me-up, she thought. She and Earl just gelled in the right way and it was wonderful to sing with him. Basil had asked her if she'd think about doing 'Over the Rainbow' with Earl but so far she'd dismissed the idea. However, during the break she'd mentioned it to him and Earl told her it was one of his favourite songs.

'My little sister died two years ago and it was her favourite song too,' she said.

His dark eyes clouded. 'I'm sorry,' he said quietly. 'What was your sister's name?'

'Betty,' Bella replied. 'She was only five years old.'

Earl reached for her hand across the table and squeezed it. This time Bella didn't pull away. 'Then let's sing it for Betty,' he suggested. 'It would make me feel real proud that we were doing that.'

'Would it?' Bella smiled.

'Sure would.'

Back onstage and after a medley of Christmas songs that the audience sang along to, Bella's heart filled with love for her lovely little Betty when Earl announced the final number.

'This next song is for a pretty little lady no longer here, but who resides in the arms of our Lord, over and beyond the rainbow,' he announced, and turned to the pianist, who gave him a nod. Bella guessed he'd had a word with him earlier. She took a deep breath and tried not to think of last Christmas Eve when Bobby's hand had crept into hers while they sang. The emotional tide she was currently on carried her along and Earl's voice, deeper than Bobby's but just as melodic, harmonised with hers. They finished to tumultuous applause, loud whistling, stamping of feet and shouts of 'More!'

'Let's give 'em "The Twelve Days of Christmas",' Earl suggested, his face splitting with the biggest smile. 'Then we can enjoy the after-party before hitting the hay.'

Everyone joined in, including the rest of the acts, and as the troupe filed offstage afterwards they all agreed it was one of the best shows they'd ever done.

'That will be a hard act to follow,' Basil said as he handed out drinks in the NAAFI. 'I wish we could take you with us, Earl.'

'Me too, buddy,' Earl said, looking at Bella. 'When you next come back this way I'll be ready and waiting to join in. Say, Basil, did I hear you mention a show planned for a Liverpool theatre in the next couple of months?'

'There is. We'll be at the Empire on Lime Street in February, if it's still standing,' Basil said. 'So far so good, mind.'

'Then in that case, and if I'm not overseas, I would be proud to join you again.'

'I'll be in touch with you before then,' Basil said. He pointed across the room. 'There's a bloke over there taking some photographs with a flash camera. I'll just go and have a word and see if he'll come and get a good one of the girls with you. When he takes the film to be developed, I'll ask him to get copies of the picture for us as well. We can pick them up the next time we're at Burtonwood. Or you can bring them over to Liverpool.'

*

Mary turned over in bed and looked across at her sleeping daughter in the narrow bed next to hers. Christmas morning and her family of five was now down to just her and Molly. Still, as far as she was aware, they were all safe. Harry over in France, and Bella in Warrington for now. They'd all be thinking of each other and remembering the last Christmas they'd spent together before little Betty died. Mary swallowed the lump in her throat. She couldn't even visit Betty's grave today. Fran's mam had promised to put a bit of greenery on for her this week, so it was better than nothing to be going on with. Molly stirred and opened her sleepy brown eyes.

'Morning, Mol,' Mary greeted her daughter.

'Morning, Mam. What time is it?'

'Just gone seven. I think the little ones are up already. I can hear excited voices. Shall we go down and see if Father Christmas has been for them? Bless them. We have to try and give them some normality. Wherever she is, their mam must be breaking her heart today, wondering if her little ones are okay. I know how I feel about my Betty. But to think of any kiddie of mine being away and not being able to be with them would be more than I could bear.' Mary slid out of bed, pulled on her dressing gown and slid her feet into her slippers. Molly slipped a warm cardigan over her pyjamas and the pair crept downstairs.

In the large farmhouse kitchen a fire blazed in the grate and a decorated pine tree stood in one alcove. Three little boys, two blond and one ginger, jigged from foot to foot with excitement.

'Look, Aunty Mary,' the little ginger-haired one cried. 'He's been, Faver Chwistmas has been.'

'Has he, Georgie?' Mary said, laughing. 'And did he eat the biscuit you left him?'

'Yes, he did and Rudolph ate the carrot as well.'

Ruth Jones, the farmer's wife, turned from the stove where she was busy stirring a large pan of porridge and smiled. 'I had to send 'em back to bed at four and again at five,' she said, shaking her head. 'Bless 'em, eh? Sit down at the table, boys, and eat your porridge and then when Uncle Bertie gets back from his milking we can all open our presents. Come on now, up you get.'

Mary helped twins Eric and Tony up on to the bench-style seats. They were only three years old and Georgie was nearly five. Three little brothers, evacuated from down near the docks in Liverpool. So far there had been no news of their mother since the area had been flattened by Nazi bombers in the blitz in May. Their father was in France and their mother had still been living in the family home as far as anyone knew. No one in authority had been able to tell them anything different.

Ruth, whose two teenage sons were away fighting with their regiment, had told Mary that if no one came to claim the boys after the war had finished, whenever that might be, she would happily take on the responsibility and bring them up as her own. She'd had them over a year now and she was fond of them. Mary thought how kind of Ruth to offer to care for them if there was no alternative.

'Mary, come on, you and Molly get yours and then we can make room for the next sitting.' Ruth laughed. 'A woman's work, and all that.' The three land girls who lived in the converted barn on the farm would be in at eight for their breakfasts. Apart from the cows being milked there was no work being done outside today. After a visit to the local church in Conwy for the morning service, the day would be spent relaxing and enjoying a Christmas dinner in front of a roaring fire and then listening to the king's speech at three o'clock.

Mary hoped Bella would get a decent dinner today. Her daughter had told her they'd be spending most of the day in the NAAFI and from what Mary had heard, the army and air-force cooks were reported to be excellent. All in all it was better than spending time in Liverpool at the mercy of whatever Hitler decided to do next. It was beyond Mary to understand how one man could get away with so many atrocities, and with everyone after him, why was he still ruling the roost? She'd never wished anyone dead in her life, but by God she wished Hitler a long, slow and very painful ending. He was an evil swine who deserved nothing less.

Chapter Twenty-One

Liverpool, March 1942

The Bryant Sisters stared up at the brightly coloured advertisement on the wall at the front of the Empire Theatre, their mouths wide with shock. They'd been told it was happening, but it was still a breathtaking moment to see their names on that poster.

'That's us,' Bella whispered. 'Us and George Formby – on the same show and at the Empire of all places. Oh my God. Can you believe it, girls?'

Fran shook her head. 'Quite honestly? No, but isn't it fantastic.'

Basil came outside to greet them. A taxi had picked them up from Fran's mother's place, where the ENSA bus had dropped them off for a quick visit, just in time to begin the rehearsal for tonight's show. Earl and several members of the Earl Franklin Junior band would be joining them shortly. The bus had gone over to Burtonwood to pick them and their instruments up.

Bella was looking forward to seeing Earl again and singing with him. He'd asked if he could write to her and they'd exchanged a couple of letters, but travelling around meant that collecting post was, as always, a bit hit and miss. Even so, it had been lovely to read his chatty news and to learn that several more American servicemen had swelled the ranks of Burtonwood. Each day more arrived throughout the country and were proving popular with English women at the various dances organised by church halls and campsites to make the troops feel welcome.

In his letters Earl had told Bella a little about his background. He'd been born and bred in New Orleans to South African immigrant parents and he was the middle son of five brothers, and one older sister whom he appeared to be very close to. His father was a jazz pianist who worked in local bars and clubs to support his family, and his mother sang alongside him. They had encouraged all their children to learn to play at least one instrument. Earl had written that New Orleans was the best place to grow up if you wanted to follow a musical career. One day, he told her, he'd like to take her there to meet his family.

Bella had felt a little thrill run through her when she'd read his letter, but really, she hardly knew him and it would be unlikely that they would be able to get together here very often, never mind in America. This wasn't the time to be making plans. Still, it was nice to have dreams and who knew what the future would bring. He'd finished his letters with 'I can't get you out of my mind and looking forward to seeing you again, All my love, Earl xxx'. She'd felt unable to confide in him about Bobby yet, but maybe one day she would.

'Right, ladies,' Basil said, breaking Bella's thoughts. 'Let's get you inside and ready to rehearse.'

'Is George Formby already here?' Fran asked.

'He's in his dressing room,' Basil replied. 'He's staying at the Adelphi Hotel up there.' He nodded in the direction of the top of Lime Street. 'We'll all be staying there tonight, Hitler willing. Nice treat for you. There's been a bit of damage to it but it's safe and still open.'

'Blimey,' Edie said. 'It's proper posh in there. Grand folk like royalty usually stop there, not the likes of us.'

Basil smiled. 'When you're next to the top of the bill at the Empire,' he said, pointing at the poster, 'I think you can safely say you're as good as anyone else that walks through its front doors.'

They laughed and followed him inside the theatre.

*

Praying there would be no air raid tonight, Bella slipped her new dress over her head. Deep burgundy lace, with a sweetheart neckline, full skirt and long sleeves, it looked and felt fabulous. Fran and Edie's were identical to hers. Their troupe seamstress had been given a bale of the fabric and she'd been hard at work, making their new outfits for this special night. The show was being put on to raise money for various good causes that would help the people of Liverpool who had been left homeless and with nothing but the clothes they stood up in. Church halls had opened their doors to provide temporary accommodation, but sleeping bags and blankets were needed as well as decent second-hand clothes and shoes. Every seat in the theatre had been sold and hopefully the money raised would help to provide some of the things needed to keep people safe and warm.

A knock at the door made them jump. Basil popped his head around it as Fran called 'Come in.' He was accompanied by Earl, who gave a low whistle and grinned, his even white teeth gleaming against his dark skin.

'You all look fabulous, ladies,' Basil said, beaming.

'You do indeed,' Earl agreed. 'And if that rehearsal was anything to go by, you'll knock 'em dead tonight. If Hitler don't do it first,' he added and then held up his hands. 'Only joking. You girls look wonderful. I'm proud to be working with you. You sure knock our Andrews Sisters into a cocked hat.'

Bella smiled. That was praise coming from a Yank; they tended to hold the Andrews Sisters in high regard. 'Thank you.'

*

Mary helped to put the little boys to bed and then went back downstairs to the kitchen, where a mug of tea waited on the table for her.

'Just poured,' Ruth announced. 'I heard you saying goodnight to them so knew you'd be down right away. Are you okay, Mary? You look a bit mithered.'

Mary took a seat at the big scrubbed pine table and picked up her mug. She took a welcome sip and sighed. 'I'm fine, chuck. Just hoping it all goes well tonight for my girl, Bella. She's written to me to tell me she's in a big show at the Empire Theatre in our city centre with George Formby. What I'd give to see that. I'm so proud of her and her pals. They've come such a long way since they used to sing together in the school choir. Who'd have thought it, eh?'

Ruth smiled. 'Oh, now that is something to be proud about.' She pointed a finger at some envelopes on the table. 'There's a letter in that lot for you. Bertie's just dropped them in. He'd been down to the village to take some eggs to the shop and Bessie was sorting through the day's delivery. That's the trouble with no regular postman now. All the young fellas from the village joined up and the women are too busy with families, farm work and evacuees to take on a post round. Still, we know where to go to pick them up so it's better than nothing. We're lucky we still get a delivery to the post office every few days.'

Mary rooted through the envelopes. She recognised her friend Ethel Hardy's writing and smiled. It was good to get regular news from the Wavertree area thanks to Ethel. She took the sheets of paper from the envelope and started to read. The first page was filled with Ethel's usual gossip about people from work and the neighbours and how she was sick to the back teeth of rationing. But the last page shocked Mary to the core:

I'm so sorry to be the bearer of bad news, Mary, but as you know the family, I thought you'd like to know that Fenella's husband, Wing Commander Harrison, has been killed in a night-time air raid over London. Their son Robert was also on the flight and has been seriously injured and is in hospital

*with very bad burns and a leg amputation. They say his
chances of survival are slim but I'm not sure how true that is
as this news has been passed on to me by someone you and I
are both acquainted with from the church.*

Mary dropped the letter onto the table and put her hand to
her mouth.

'Is it bad news?' Ruth asked.

Mary nodded, her eyes filling. 'A friend's husband has been
killed and their son seriously injured. Young Bobby was Bella's
boyfriend for a while. I don't know how I'm going to tell her this
news. She'll be heartbroken. It doesn't sound good for him either.
He's lost a leg and has got serious burns.'

'Oh dear. Poor lad. And what about the wife, your friend? Is
she okay?'

Mary realised she hadn't given Fenella a thought, or Alicia
come to that. 'I don't know. Ethel doesn't say. She'll be very upset
of course. I'll write back tonight and ask Ethel to find out how she
is. I can't write to my friend because she's staying in Oxfordshire
near to where the men were stationed at Brize Norton and I don't
have an address.'

Ruth nodded. 'You could always send a letter care of the camp
to be forwarded to her.'

'Now that's a thought. I might just do that.' Mary left the table
and took Ethel's letter up to her room. She'd write back later when
she'd finished helping with the evening chores. She'd have to let Bella
know about Bobby and that thought didn't fill her with pleasure.

*

The Bryant Sisters stood in the wings, anxiously awaiting their cue
to go onstage. Earl and his band were currently warming up the
audience with a couple of Glenn Miller instrumentals. The girls
jigged and swayed from side to side to the melody of 'Little Brown

Jug'. Then Earl was at the edge of the stage announcing them and they squeezed hands and ran on to a great cheer from the audience. Earl had introduced them as Liverpool's own Andrews Sisters. They took a bow and as the band launched into 'Don't Fence Me In', Bella felt all her concerns at performing in such an important show vanish and she gave herself to the music. This was a dream come true for her and momentarily she wished that Bobby could have been here to see her and to share in the trio's success. But Earl's twinkling brown eyes and smiles of admiration spurred her on and she pushed the thoughts away. Bobby had let her down. Hopefully Earl wouldn't. When this war was over and they could pick up the pieces of their previous lives again, there might be some hope for all of them.

George Formby closed the second half of the show and the audience went wild. He called the girls onstage to join him. He nodded at Earl, who was seated at the piano. Earl played the opening chords to 'Leaning on a Lamp-post' and George stuck his thumb in the air and picked up his ukulele. 'Ready, ladies?' They all joined in and then George suggested they finish the night with a Vera Lynn song. 'You take lead vocals,' he said to Bella. The audience sang along to 'We'll Meet Again'.

Bella felt waves of emotion washing over her and gave the song her all. She couldn't believe she was standing next to George Formby in her home city singing one of her favourite songs. Wait until she wrote to Mam and Molly with an update to tell them how the show went. She reached for Fran and Edie's hands, knowing how much this song would mean to them until Frankie and Stevie were safely home. And once more Bobby's face flashed into her mind. If only things could have been different.

Chapter Twenty-Two

The after-party at The Adelphi Hotel came to an abrupt end when the air raid sirens sounded loud and clear. The sky had been clear and starlit with a full moon, a perfect night for Jerry bombers to descend on the city. Grabbing their handbags and the ever-present gas mask boxes, the weary artistes shuffled to the air raid shelters in the basement of the building.

At least it was more comfortable than the shelters on the streets and for that Bella was grateful. She hoped the planes droning low overhead now would avoid Wavertree and leave them with homes to return to eventually. The dull thuds that shook the city meant somewhere close by wasn't so lucky. There wasn't much left to destroy. The lovely buildings known as the Three Graces down by the dockside had miraculously escaped any major damage so far and Bella hoped they'd be missed tonight as well.

Earl squeezed into the place next to her.

'You okay, honey?' he whispered. 'What a way to spend the last few hours of a fabulous evening.'

Bella nodded. 'I'm fine thanks. But that's just typical of Hitler. Always spoils the party.'

Earl smiled. 'You guys are sure getting some hammer in this poor city. I saw some of the damage as we drove to the theatre. Some beautiful buildings hanging in by a thread.'

'I know. It's such a pity you're not getting to see it at its best. We have some lovely areas and parks.'

Earl nodded. 'I'm not going back to camp until late afternoon tomorrow and I don't think you girls will be going until after we've been taken back and the bus is free. Why don't you show me some parts that are still standing?'

Bella smiled. 'Okay, I'd love to. Maybe if there are trams running we can go over to my old home and I can check that it's still standing. I promised Mam in a letter that I would do that if I could. There's a lovely park over there and a little café nearby where we can get a cuppa.'

'It's a date,' Earl said.

'Is it?' Bella looked at him. His face was serious for once.

'It is if you want it to be.'

She smiled. 'Then a date it is.'

Earl slipped his arm around her and pulled her closer. Bella leaned into him. It felt comfortable and he smelled nice. He was wearing cologne that smelled sort of woody and spicy. She liked it. Her eyes felt heavy and she struggled to stay awake. It had been a big day; she felt exhausted and the two schooners of after-show sherry had taken their toll too.

Fran and Edie were chatting to some members of Earl's band and no one was looking at her, so she snuggled in a bit closer and Earl's arms tightened around her. She looked up into his eyes. He bent his head and dropped a kiss on the end of her nose. She lifted her face to his and his lips met hers in a gentle kiss. It made her tummy tingle and she responded, kissing him back. Earl kissed her again, harder this time, and Bella was glad they were surrounded by people as she just might have chucked her inhibitions to the wind, the feelings he was giving her. She pulled away and stared at him.

'Honey, what are you doing to me?' he whispered.

She shook her head in reply, lost for words. She didn't know, but whatever his feelings she was sure they matched hers.

'I have to see you again, for sure. Tomorrow and on our own. Yes?'

'Yes,' she whispered. 'After breakfast. Meet me in the foyer around half past nine. I'll tell Fran and Edie I'm popping out on a bit of business for my mam. Otherwise, if I tell them I'm going home they'll want to come along as they live close by me.' As she finished, the air raid sirens sounded the end of the raid and, as people got to their feet, Earl stole another quick kiss and squeezed her tight.

'I'll be waiting.'

Bella and Earl alighted from the tram on Picton Road and Bella led him towards The Mystery Park. He was intrigued by the name and she explained to him how it had received it.

'Wow, so the guy just gave it to the town in secret? What a great thing to do. It's pretty too. Look at all those flowers, beautiful colours.'

'Daffodils and crocuses, spring flowers,' Bella said. 'I love this time of the year. Such a shame the air is tainted with the smell of burning. Somewhere close by must have copped it bad last night. Hope no one was badly hurt.'

They'd had a quick stroll around part of the city, but a lot of streets were cordoned off where buildings were falling down or being demolished as they were beyond repair. She would like to have taken Earl across the Mersey on a ferry to New Brighton, but the docks had been damaged yet again last night and it wasn't a safe place right now. New Brighton had also suffered a lot of damage, so it wasn't in the best state to show it off. Maybe when the war was over he could visit England and then she would show him all her favourite places.

'Let's see if we can get a cuppa at the café,' she suggested after they'd had a good stroll around. At one point he'd spotted the grand houses on Prince Alfred Road and said they looked nice. She told him a friend used to live in one and they were lovely inside. 'I can't make you a drink at home because there's nothing in to make it with. Mam emptied the cupboards before she left.'

The café was open but empty and Bella was glad about that. An elderly couple walking a small dog had passed them by and raised their eyebrows. Bella had turned round and spotted them staring after them. She wasn't ashamed to be seen holding the hand of a man as handsome as Earl and to her it didn't matter what colour his skin was. He was a really nice person and she felt comfortable with him. As they sat at a table near the window with tea and a slice of sponge cake each, he pulled out his wallet and took a postcard-sized photo from the back.

'This is my family,' he said. 'Ma and Pa and', he pointed at each one in turn, Monty, Levi, Ruby, me, Eddie and Scotty. Taken about five years ago, but it's the only one with us all that I could bring with me.'

Bella smiled as she looked at the family. All had their parents' good looks and broad smiles, and those fine cheekbones and gleaming white teeth. 'What a handsome family. Your sister is beautiful. I love her hair.' Ruby's long locks fell in tight ringlets past her shoulders. 'Mam used to fasten our hair up in rags at night to try and get ringlets, but all we got was a headache and waves.'

Earl laughed. 'Ruby never stops messing with her hair. She'd love waves like yours but there ain't no way that curly mop will ever be wavy.'

'Are you close to them all?'

He nodded. 'Ruby is my best pal. She's my confidante.'

Bella wondered if he'd mentioned her to his family in letters home yet. Would they approve of their son getting involved with an English girl? And also what would Mam say? The girls had all been given a copy of the photo that had been taken on Christmas Eve after the show at Burtonwood. Bella had to admit that they all looked great together, very professional; and Earl was right by her side and his expression as he looked at her spoke volumes.

Mam would be sure to guess that there was an attraction between them. Her friend Ethel's late husband Bernie had been from the West Indies and she'd always got on well with him until he was hit by a train while at work and died instantly. Mam wasn't prejudiced, which was a good thing, but Bella decided it may be best not to send her a copy of the photo just yet. 'Have you finished?' she asked as he put down his cup. 'Shall we go and take a look around my house now? Just to make sure everything is all right, then I can let Mam know when I write to her later.'

Earl nodded. 'Lead the way.'

As they strolled out of the café Bella pointed to a bed of daffodils. 'They've just reminded me, I know what else I'd like to do while we're here.' She grabbed Earl's hand and led him away from the park and towards the row of shops near her home. Outside the greengrocer's two metal buckets of water held a variety of spring flowers neatly tied in bunches. Bella chose a mixed bunch and went inside to pay for them, leaving Earl outside looking puzzled.

'I would have bought you flowers,' he said as she rejoined him on the pavement. 'You only had to say.'

She smiled. 'They're for my sister Betty's grave. It won't take us long to walk to the churchyard.'

He looked sober and nodded as he took the bunch from her. 'I'll carry them. Pretty rainbow colours. Perfect for the little lady.'

Bella linked his arm as they hurried to the churchyard. There was a jar of dead greenery standing in the middle of the plot and Earl emptied it into a nearby dustbin.

'Is there a tap nearby where I can rinse and refill this?'

Bella pointed to a tap on a nearby wall. 'Just over there.'

She unwrapped the flowers and when Earl brought back the jar, clean and full of fresh water, she arranged them neatly and placed it on the grave. 'There, little Bets,' she said softly.

Earl slipped his arm around her waist and she laid her head on his shoulder, tears running down her cheeks.

'Man, I don't know how you coped with losing her,' Earl said softly, his voice husky with emotion. 'To lose my sister would destroy me. I hope you found a perfect rainbow to rest on, little one,' he directed at the headstone, where Betty's name was engraved in gold leaf. He took a clean white handkerchief from his pocket and wiped Bella's eyes. He dropped a kiss on top of her head and held her close. 'Shall we go and check your house now, then we should make our way back into the city ready for my lift back to base.'

Bella nodded. 'Thank you for being here. I'm not sure I could have done this on my own. I usually have Mam or Molly with me.'

'Glad to be here for you. Thank you for sharing the moment with me. It means a lot that you felt you could.' He took her hand and squeezed it tight and they made their way to the gates, Bella looking back over her shoulder and blowing a kiss.

Bella opened the front door of her home and invited Earl inside. She slid a bolt into place and smiled. 'If any of the neighbours saw us coming inside they'll be over and just walk in. It's what they do around here. I just don't feel in the mood for small talk right now.'

'I understand,' Earl said. 'It's the same in my neighbourhood back home.'

As they wandered into the back room Bella picked up a framed photo of herself, Molly and Betty and showed it to him. 'Taken the last Christmas she was here,' she told him.

'Pretty girls,' he said. 'Molly is sure like you and Betty was real cute. And you say she was just five years old?' He shook his head. For a moment there was a faraway look in his eyes and he turned away to put the photograph back on the mantelpiece.

Bella frowned, but by the time she'd wondered what he was thinking about the moment had passed and he pointed to another framed photo. 'Wedding day. Your mom and dad?'

Bella nodded.

'You all look like your dad,' he said.

'Everyone says that. I'll just go and take a look in each room to make sure there's no water leaks or anything. Have a seat, I won't be a minute. Sorry it's cold but there's been no fire lit in here for ages now.'

Earl nodded and sat down in her dad's old armchair. Bella checked in the kitchen and the front parlour and then ran up the stairs. Hers and Molly's bedroom seemed fine. No marks on the ceiling to indicate a slate had slipped, causing leaks. The curtains were closed in all the rooms to keep everywhere dark during blackout time.

She pulled one back to take a look outside, down onto the yard below. It all looked the same. There was no one around, as most of the neighbours this side of Victory Street had gone to stay with family out of Liverpool. Mam had cancelled the window cleaner and the windows were filthy. God knows what state they'd be in once the war ended, but hopefully they'd still be intact.

She opened the door to her mam's room. It had a musty smell about it, probably from being closed up for months. The bed was stripped of sheets, but a blanket and blue satin eiderdown covered the mattress to stop it getting dusty. As she walked over to the window to check the glass was still intact, from the corner of her eye Bella thought she saw something scoot under the bed.

Something brown, furry and with a tail. *A mouse? Oh my God, what if it was a rat?* She was terrified of rats and mice. She bent to peer under the bed and whatever it was looked at her, squeaked and ran towards the cast iron fireplace on the chimney breast. It vanished from sight, presumably up the chimney. She screamed at the top of her voice and jumped up onto the bed, shrieking for Earl. His feet pounded up the stairs and he shot into the room.

'What is it?' he asked, seeing her wobbling on the uneven mattress springs and trying to hold on to the wooden headboard while pointing at the fireplace and stuttering.

'Mouse,' she gasped. 'It's gone up the chimney.'

Earl scratched the top of his head and bent to look up the fireplace. 'Honey, there's nothing there,' he said, trying hard not to laugh. 'It's probably more scared than you are. May be living up in the roof space and just ventured down to stretch his legs. I can't see anything.'

'He stared me right in the eye and squeaked,' Bella said indignantly. 'Stop laughing at me.' As she saw the amused look in his eyes she started to giggle, seeing the funny side of the scenario. 'Help me down, please.' She put out her hand and as he took it, her heel got caught in the blanket and she wobbled backwards, pulling him with her. They bounced on the uneven springs, helpless with laughter.

Earl leaned up on one elbow and looked at her. 'You sure look beautiful when you're laughing,' he said, pulling her closer and dropping a kiss on her lips. She responded to his kisses and caresses. Earl made her feel like she'd never felt before and she wondered if this was what falling in love felt like.

Fran had told her that she and Frankie couldn't keep their hands off each other and right now, in Earl's arms, she understood what she had meant. As he unbuttoned her coat, Bella reached out to unfasten his jacket. Although the room was cold, here snuggled up with Earl, removing one another's clothes, she only felt the warmth from his body.

As they lay naked Earl whispered, 'Are you sure this is what you want, honey? Because I sure do. I've wanted to from the moment I met you.'

She looked into his eyes and nodded. 'More than anything,' she whispered back. 'I've never, before... well, you know.'

'Don't worry, I'll take care of you. I love you, baby.'

Bella didn't get the chance to reply as his lips came down hard on hers and she responded to his touch. Her body felt like it was on fire, like nothing she'd ever experienced before. Earl was a skilled lover and even though the thought passed quickly through her mind that he'd done this before, she was glad in a way as he taught her how to enjoy lovemaking for the first time and not be scared or embarrassed.

Afterward as they lay together, savouring the magical moment, Bella asked him, 'Did you mean it when you said you loved me?'

He nodded. 'With all my heart.'

She sighed. 'I love you too.'

He squeezed her tight and sighed into her hair. 'Bella, with this war raging I don't know what the future holds for us, or where I'll be sent with my squadron eventually, but I'll come back for you, no matter how long it takes, I'll be back for you. There's a lot of mess to sort out, me being a Yank and you an English girl, but promise you'll be my girl and wait for me.'

Bella felt tears welling in her eyes. This bloody war had a lot to answer for. 'I promise.'

As they sat on the almost deserted tram going back into the city centre, Earl looked at his watch. 'We'll just about make it,' he said. 'Thank you for the best first date I've ever had in my life. I wasn't expecting it, you know. That took me by surprise. You don't regret it, do you?'

'Not for one moment,' Bella replied, squeezing his hand. 'I hate having to say goodbye to you, not knowing when we'll get a chance to see each other again. We're at Burtonwood again in a few weeks' time. Hopefully you'll be there with your band and not out on manoeuvres. But I'll write when I can, and you do the same. At some point we'll get each other's letters.'

At the Adelphi the bus was already waiting. Basil called out to Earl to hurry up and that all his stuff was on board. Earl waved his hand and pulled Bella into his arms for one last kiss. The driver hooted impatiently and Earl climbed on to the bus platform, giving her one last wave. She blew him a kiss as the bus pulled away.

Fran and Edie were standing with Basil and beckoned her over. Basil moved away to talk to one of the other acts.

'Where've you been?' Edie said, smiling at her. 'We've been looking all over for you.'

'I've just been showing Earl some of the city, and er, we popped over to Wavertree to put some flowers on Betty's grave and to check the house for Mam.'

'Did you now?' Fran said, looking closely at Bella's flushed face. 'You two in an empty house. Oh my God.' She lowered her voice. 'It's written all over your face. You've done the deed.'

Bella felt her cheeks heating. 'I love him,' she whispered. 'He loves me. It felt right. We don't know what sort of future any of us have got. I might never see him again.' Her voice broke and she hated thinking along those lines.

Fran rubbed her arm. 'I know what you mean. We have to take happiness where we can. But seriously, Bella, how can it work? He's a Yank, he's black. You might get a lot of prejudice chucked at you. I wish you both the best of luck, but you'll need to grow a tough skin, girl.'

Edie nodded. 'But no matter what, Fran and I are here for you and we always will be. We love Earl. Not in the same way as you, obviously, but he's a lovely man and so talented. I hope things work out for you both.'

'Thank you. I appreciate that,' Bella said and gave them both a hug.

Chapter Twenty-Three

Basil handed out the post he'd just collected from one of the points of pick-up on the way over to Yorkshire. They'd left Liverpool and had stayed at the digs in Didsbury for a two-day break and rehearsals in the church hall before leaving this morning. The troupe were to stay at Catterick camp for a few days, entertaining the soldiers, before moving on up to Scotland.

They'd stopped for a drink and a sandwich at a tea shop. Bella had two letters, one from Mam and the other from Molly. Mam's had been sent before the one Bella had posted yesterday, telling her the house was fine and that she'd put flowers on Betty's grave. It was most unusual for Mam to send extra letters as she usually waited for one to respond to. Bella tore the envelope open, hoping the letter wouldn't say there was something wrong or she'd decided she wanted to come home. She had peace of mind while Mam was out of the city with Molly. It was much easier to cope with.

As she scanned the letter and saw the line 'sorry I have to be the bearer of this very sad news', her heart skipped a beat and her stomach turned over, thinking something had happened to her dad. As she read further her hand flew to her mouth. Bobby's father had been killed and Bobby was seriously injured. She dropped the letter onto the table and burst into tears.

'Bella, what is it? What's happened?' Fran said.

Bella pointed at the letter. 'Read it,' she sobbed.

Fran reached across the table and picked up the letter. 'Oh my God,' she said, showing it to Edie. 'Oh that's awful.'

Bella nodded. 'Bobby could be dead now for all I know,' she cried. 'Mam's written to his mother but is waiting for a reply. How can I find out if he's all right?'

Seeing his girls so upset, Basil came over to the table. 'What's wrong?'

Fran read him the contents of Bella's mam's letter.

'Oh lord, that *is* bad news. Poor lad.' He paused for a moment. 'We're back at Brize Norton about July. When we get to Catterick I'll make some calls. Try and find out how Bobby is doing. Such a shame about his father. I met him a while ago. He was a nice bloke. This bloody war. We're losing some of our bravest and best.' He patted Bella on the shoulder. 'Try not to worry, love. I'll do my best.'

Lying on her camp bed in the allocated Nissan hut, Bella couldn't stop thinking about Bobby. Badly burned, Mam had said, and he'd lost a leg too. It broke her heart to think of him in such a horrific accident. He'd be in such a state about losing his father as they were very close, never mind his leg. She hoped it wasn't his lovely face that was burnt. *What if he dies before I can see him?*

She had no idea how long ago the accident had happened as Mam said her news came via a letter from Ethel Hardy, who'd related it second-hand. If she could find out which hospital he was being treated in she would write to him. Alicia wouldn't be able to get her hands on it before Bobby saw it then. Hopefully Basil would come up with something tomorrow when he could get to use the phone and talk to his contact at Brize Norton.

She realised that since getting Mam's letter she hadn't even given Earl a thought, and felt bad about it. That didn't feel right as he was now her lover and sweetheart, she'd promised to wait for him, and her thoughts should be on him and him alone. Bobby had let her down, but if it hadn't been for Alicia and her underhanded ways Bella would be Bobby's fiancée by now, or even his wife.

She almost felt she'd been unfaithful to him and it was just silly to feel that way, but she couldn't help it. She did still love Bobby, she knew that, he was her first love, her childhood sweetheart, but it was a different kind of love to the passionate and all-consuming afternoon she'd spent with Earl. She'd always thought Bobby would be the only one and she would have waited until their wedding day.

Bobby was the sort of boy who would have been happy to do that for her, even though he'd jumped the gun with Alicia – she'd bet her life he hadn't been the instigator there. But on that afternoon with Earl, she'd wanted to as much as he did. It was almost as though she'd been driven to feel as though she belonged to him after being let down by Bobby. Why was everything such a muddle in her head?

She turned onto her side and closed her eyes. Fran and Edie had been flat out for ages after a good meal in the NAAFI and a couple of games of cards with some of the soldiers. She needed to sleep as they had a full day of rehearsals tomorrow and she had to be fresh and lively for that. Keeping up the troops' morale was the most important thing for now.

Halfway through rehearsals in the NAAFI Basil took Bella to one side and handed her a slip of paper. Written on it were the details of Bobby's ward and the address of a London hospital, including a phone number.

'So he's still alive then?' she whispered, her voice trembling.

'He is, love. The guy I spoke to is my contact for putting the shows on at Benson and Brize Norton. He was over at Brize when I got hold of him. The wing commander's funeral is to be held in Liverpool soon. Mrs Harrison is in a bad way apparently. Bobby's wife went with her to see him but has refused to go again. Can't bear to see him in that state, so she says.'

Bella raised an eyebrow.

'Well quite. She's back working at the camp and my mate thinks there's something going on with another airman. He's seen her making eyes at him on a regular basis when she's been handing out the post to the lads, and the making eyes is reciprocated.' Bella looked furious and Basil rushed on before she could interrupt. 'I suggest you drop Bobby a line, let him know we're all thinking about him. Let's try and keep his morale up, because he'll be discharged from the RAF now. He might not be able to fly planes, but when he's fit for working in the future, he can still sing with us, even in a wheelchair.'

'Oh bless you Basil, I'll do that.'

'Give him some hope to hang on to, Bella. You and he made a good team. As soon as we're near enough to London I'll get someone to run you there to see him, that's if they don't transfer him nearer to home, and even then we'll still get you a visit. I can always come with you if you feel you need me to.' Basil patted her on the shoulder and went across to talk to someone who was calling his name.

Bella took a deep breath and slipped the paper into her pocket. She'd write a letter to Bobby later and get it sent off as soon as she could. What Basil said about Bobby joining them at a later date made sense and would help give him a sense of purpose. She strolled across to Fran and Edie, who were talking to a couple of soldiers, one blond, one dark-haired.

'These two make a good cuppa,' Fran announced as Bella sat down at the table. 'They bake a nice cake as well.'

'Would you like a brew, love?' the blond lad asked. 'And Danny here will get you a slice of his world-famous Victoria sponge.'

'Oh please,' Bella said.

'We might not be outside fighting any battles, but you know what they say,' Danny said. 'An army marches on its stomach!'

'Indeed it does.' Bella smiled as they walked over to the counter for her snack. She showed Fran and Edie the paper Basil had given her and told her of his suggestion about giving Bobby support and how Alicia had only visited him once.

'The rotten bitch,' Fran retorted. 'If she was at all worried about him, she'd be staying in a hotel nearby and visiting as often she could. Not back at work for the WAAF and bloody miles away. And she's flirting with another bloke, Basil says? God Bella, I could scratch her eyes out. You and Bobby were so happy until she came on the scene. And now look, you're involved with Earl as well and we all know that one will end up a disaster. What a bloody mix-up.'

'Why will me and Earl end up a disaster? We get along fine and his latest letter is lovely. I'm very fond of Bobby, you all know that. And if we can help him look towards some sort of future in time then we will do. But he's still married, no matter what. I'll write to him and I will visit him when I can. But we'll have to see what happens next. Meantime, I'm going to enjoy my tea and cake. Thank you, boys,' she said to the two young cooks, who had brought a tray over and placed it in front of her. 'Anyway, Earl's my boyfriend now. We've committed to each other.'

Fran shook her head. 'Sleeping with a bloke once does not make a commitment. Neither does a letter full of what might be lies.'

'Fran,' Edie said. 'What's wrong with you? Why are you saying that?'

Fran got to her feet. 'Oh just ignore me. I'm tired and I don't want to see Bella getting hurt again, that's all. I'm going to the toilet.' She strode away, leaving Bella and Edie staring after her.

Bella shrugged her shoulders. 'Maybe she's right. Time will tell. We'll just have to see what happens. But I'm not putting all my eggs in one basket this time.'

'Anyway, enough about me. What have you heard from Stevie?'

Edie smiled, a dreamy look in her eyes. 'He's fine. Somewhere out in France, but he can't tell me where of course. It's just so nice to hear from him.'

'You really like him, don't you?'

'I do. I never thought I'd ever meet anyone that felt so right, having only met him that once. But we seem to have a lot in common. Time will tell.'

Bobby's quick response to Bella's letter came as a surprise. She'd been expecting it to take him forever, if he even wrote back at all. But in less than a week, on their way to Scotland, Basil handed her an envelope containing several sheets of handwritten paper.

My dear Bella,

I cannot tell you how happy I was to receive your lovely and much-welcomed letter. The last few weeks have been traumatic, to say the least. Losing my father has taken its toll on all of us. Mother is inconsolable as you would expect.

What makes matters worse is that I was at the controls, well second in command anyway. It was only my third flight in control and will no doubt be my last. I feel distraught and responsible for my father's death. I know that's not true as Jerry shot us down, but you'll understand what I mean.

Anyway, that besides, I'm in a bit of a mess to say the least. I won't go into it but at least I can still see and hear and smell, so my senses, for what they are worth, are still intact, as I hope is my sense of humour. Mother and Alicia came to see me a while ago but Alicia hasn't been back.

One thing I'm sure of: there was no baby, Bella. She tricked me, only three days after the wedding she said she was miscarrying but the doctor who came out to see her said she wasn't pregnant and that it was just the normal monthly thing you women get.

I still love you and I always will. I hope that with you writing to me this means that we can still be friends, at least. I need you in my life Bella. Please help me to get through this mess. And one day, when this war is over and I can get a divorce, we might be able to be more than that. Just reading in your letter that we may be able to sing together again has given me hope that I might have a future, if not as your husband, at least as your singing partner, which is more than I could have hoped for.

Please write back to me as soon as you can and visit when you are near London. I will let you know as soon as I can if they decide to transfer me to a convalescent home when my burns are improving. I've asked for one near Liverpool if possible. Thank you Bella for giving me some hopes back. All my love, Bobby. Xxx

Bella read and reread Bobby's letter with tears streaming down her cheeks. Poor Bobby. And that bloody Alicia needed horse-whipping, as her mam would say. How callous and unfeeling of her. And Mam was right after all, as were Fran and Edie. There never was a baby. She folded the letter and put it in her handbag. She'd write back to him later. She needed to write to Earl as well when she had a minute.

With the Scottish shows out of the way, the ENSA troupe headed back towards their home territory of Liverpool, although they were staying in Didsbury at the usual digs. Time was flying, they seemed to be working harder than ever and there was still no sign of the war coming to an end. Thousands of American soldiers and airmen were now living in barracks in the UK and helping with the battle. There had been talk of taking the entertainments troupe across to Europe on ships and performing on board on the way but nothing had been firmly decided yet.

Bella didn't really fancy doing that – she wasn't good on water; even crossing the Mersey on the New Brighton ferry was a struggle the odd time she'd done it. Her heart wasn't into anything much at the moment. She was still writing to Earl and although his letters were chatty and full of what he'd been doing, she felt he was a bit distant at times. Maybe, as Fran had said, she was just a bit infatuated with him, the way he could sing and dance onstage as well as the way he made her feel special when they sang together. But there was something missing, and she didn't know what it was.

On the other hand, Bobby's letters were frequent and friendly and she looked forward to receiving them and then writing back to him. She hadn't been to London yet as they hadn't been near the area, but he'd told her he was being transferred next month to a place on the Wirral, close enough to Liverpool for his mother to visit. She was now living back at her home on Prince Alfred Road and would be staying there permanently.

Of Alicia he'd had no news other than that she was still working in Oxfordshire, and he had asked his mother to instruct the family solicitor to instigate divorce proceedings.

Serves the girl right, Bella thought. So much for her professing to love Bobby. She'd made a right hash of that through her jealous behaviour, acting like a spoilt child. And now he was in a bad way, she didn't want to know.

'You okay?' Fran's voice broke into Bella's thoughts.

'Yes, I'm fine. Just feeling a bit sickly and tired for some reason, but I had a good sleep last night,' Bella replied.

'It's all the travelling we do and rushing to eat while we can,' Fran said. 'Not to mention broken sleep from air raids. Although we're luckier than most I suppose. 'Anyway, soon be near home. Then you can catch up with Bobby if they've brought him up this way yet.'

'And Earl,' Bella reminded her. 'We're in Burtonwood again next week for a show.'

Fran nodded. 'I know. I'm looking forward to sleeping in a real bed tonight. Camp beds play havoc with my poor old back. God, we're only eighteen and already I feel as old as Mam with my achy back and knees.'

Bella frowned. 'You've been saying your back hurts for a while, Fran. Why don't you get one of the doctors at Burtonwood to examine you, make sure you haven't pulled a muscle or hurt a disc or something?'

'Hmm, I might do that. I'll see how I feel after a night on a proper mattress. I'll take a couple of aspirins before I go to bed.'

Chapter Twenty-Four

RAF Burtonwood, Warrington, June 1942

For the second morning in a row, Bella refused breakfast. She sat at the table in the Didsbury digs dining room, hugging a mug of tea and fighting the feeling of nausea that washed over her if she so much as dared to move. She was conscious of Fran looking closely at her. She avoided her eyes, because if Fran voiced her thoughts, Bella would have to face up to what she pretty much knew was wrong.

Fran pushed a plate of toast towards her. 'Try a bit. You need something inside you before we go shopping.' The trio had planned to visit Manchester city centre to see if they could get new lipsticks from Lewis's store, as Liverpool's was currently closed while it was made safe after the blitz attacks.

Bella pulled her face. 'I can't. I'm fine with this tea. I'll get something while we're out.' She indicated a dish of scrambled eggs on the table. 'I don't like the powdered eggs,' she said. 'We've been spoiled with all the fresh ones we get at the camps.'

'Tell me about it,' Edie said, although she was shovelling forkfuls into her mouth as though enjoying it. 'It's so dry, but better than nowt. And I'm starving.'

Bella smiled weakly. 'I'll just go back upstairs while you two finish eating. See you in a bit.' She left the dining room, conscious of

Fran staring at her back. She hurried upstairs to the large bedroom the threesome shared and sat down on the bed. Her handbag was on the floor by the bed and she took her diary from inside, reluctantly opening the pages.

She counted again, knowing it wouldn't be any different to yesterday's count. She'd had no monthlies since March, since before she and Earl had made love, and now it was June. There was no other reason for feeling like she did; she was carrying Earl's baby. She lay back on the bed, feeling tears run down her face and on to the counterpane beneath her head. They weren't tears of joy either. More like tears of despair.

The bedroom door opened and Fran and Edie walked in. Bella shuffled up the bed to let them sit down, and pulled herself into a sitting position. She gagged, jumped up and shot out of the room praying no one was in the bathroom. Thankfully it was empty: she dropped to her knees and retched up the tea she'd just drunk. Exhausted, she flushed the toilet and rinsed her face and mouth at the sink. She looked in the mirror on the windowsill and sighed. Big dark circles under her eyes. Not a look that suited her.

She made her way back to the bedroom and sat back down on her bed as two pairs of curious eyes stared at her. 'I'm pregnant,' she mumbled.

'We guessed that,' Fran said, going to sit beside her. 'Oh, Bella, what are you going to do?'

Edie came and sat the other side and held her hand. 'We're here for you, you know that don't you?'

'Thank you,' Bella said, tears running down her cheeks. 'I'll have to tell Earl tomorrow. There's not much we can do, is there?'

'He could offer to marry you,' Fran said.

'Can an American marry an English girl?' Edie asked. 'Is it that simple?'

Fran shrugged. 'No idea. Don't see why not though. I tell you what, Bella: you won't be the only one. There's thousands of Yanks here now and still arriving. Maybe you could go and live in New Orleans with his family.'

Bella was horrified at the suggestion. She looped her hair behind her ears and shook her head. 'No, I don't want to marry Earl, nor do I want to go and live in America.' Saying it out loud, she realised it was true. 'I want to be here with you two, and my family. But most of all I need to be here for Bobby. Oh God, this is such a disaster. Why has this happened to me now, of all times? I can't believe it. Mam will go mad with me. I'll have to stop singing – that's letting everyone in the show down and I can't help Mam out with money if I'm not working.'

'Right.' Fran took charge. 'This needs a plan. First of all, you'll have to tell Earl tomorrow. Once you've got that out of the way, you will need to speak to Basil. You're only about three months, so you could still work for another three or four months. If you wear loose clothing no one will guess. You can get plenty of rest apart from rehearsals and stage time. We'll make sure you do. Basil won't want to let you go, I'm sure. Nearer delivery time you'll have to take a few weeks off before and after and that should do it.'

Bella shook her head. 'You think so? What do I do with a baby afterwards? Who will look after it? And how the hell do I face Bobby with this problem?'

Fran rolled her eyes. 'Well, Bobby's not as white as you paint him, is he? He got up to stuff, enough to make him marry the girl anyway. You won't be seeing much of him, so does he really need to know?'

Bella sighed. 'Maybe not. No one needs to know until the last few weeks, apart from Earl, and Basil of course. That gives me time to have a good think about things. I can't believe I'm thinking this far ahead, but maybe the kindest thing to do would be to give the baby up for adoption, although I don't know if I can bear that. But I won't be able to support it unless I can work and that means being away all the time. Let's see what happens tomorrow. I might feel better about all of this once I've seen Earl again.'

*

Earl had arrived back from his training duties mid-afternoon, halfway through rehearsals. He joined the Bryant Sisters onstage and they performed a medley of songs for that night's show. He greeted everyone with a friendly hug and kiss and Bella didn't feel his hug was any more special for her than it was for Fran and Edie. She felt a bit churned up at seeing him again, but singing along with him there was definitely that extra spark, which made her feel better. He grabbed her hand and squeezed it as they sang a duet.

'I've some form-filling-in duties to attend to; I'll see you all here later,' he said afterwards. He dashed away, leaving Bella staring after him. Fran linked her arm and they made their way to a table where refreshments were being laid out.

'You okay?'

Bella nodded. 'After the show, maybe I'll get the chance to talk to him alone.'

'You need to make that chance,' Fran said. 'He seemed a bit unsure of himself, just then, don't you think? Could be because you haven't seen him for a while. Or maybe he's just tired from training practices. Who knows?'

Bella's head was in a whirl. She still felt a bit queasy, although as the day wore on the feelings lessened. Her mind was on Bobby and how she would be visiting him soon in the convalescent home on the Wirral. It was going to be hard to try to keep her face from registering shock seeing him in a wheelchair with just one leg.

It saddened her to think of her childhood friend like that. The times they'd run races at school, danced together, watching him play cricket with his pals on The Mystery Park with no worries about his future; singing with her at Speke Legion with not a care in the world. And at just eighteen he'd got a broken marriage behind him, had lost his father and survived a plane crash but was crippled for life.

He'd told her in his latest letter how much pain he was in while the burns healed. That there was always a risk of infection setting him back months. Poor Bobby. Her heart went out to him – and here she was with her life in a total mess and not knowing which way to turn.

At the after-party that night, Earl led Bella to a secluded part of the NAAFI and gave her a kiss. 'You okay, honey? You've been awful quiet today. Is something wrong? I've been looking forward to seeing you again for weeks, but you seem a bit distant.'

Bella smiled and sat down at the small table with her back to everyone else in the room. She gestured for Earl to take a seat too. 'I'm okay. But we need to talk.' She saw a look of panic cross his face and his brown eyes, and almost lost her nerve.

'We do?' He raised a questioning eyebrow. 'Have you met someone else, Bella? Am I about to get the Dear John letter in person? I guess that's better than through the mail.'

'What? Oh no, Earl. No. I need to tell you something.'

He nodded, looking puzzled. 'Go ahead.'

'I'm er…' She hesitated. What would the Yanks call it? 'I'm er, I'm expecting a baby, *your* baby, Earl.' There, she'd done it and he was looking at her like she'd gone mad. Bella felt sick. He didn't look very pleased; not that she'd been expecting him to, but a smile might have helped.

He shook his head. 'You're having my kid? Seriously? Boy, does that cause problems.'

'Does it?' She watched as he sat with his head in his hands, shaking it from side to side.

'Oh man, it sure does.'

'Why? You told me you loved me several times, including the day this happened.'

He nodded. 'I did, and Bella, I do. But, oh shit, sweetheart, I'm a married man with a five-year-old daughter, same age as your little sister was. I wasn't free to get involved with you and I shouldn't have done.'

Bella felt winded. As though someone had punched her in the guts. That wasn't what she was expecting at all. 'Then why did you?'

'Because…' He looked at her and shrugged his shoulders. 'Because I fell in love with you on sight. My marriage isn't in a good place, I can't see it lasting the war out if I'm honest, but no matter, at the moment I'm not free to make you any promises about the future.'

Bella nodded, a slight feeling of relief washing over her that he wouldn't be getting down on one knee to propose marriage. But she'd still need some support, at least. She swallowed hard. 'So, meantime, what do you suggest I do about this?' She laid her hand on her slightly rounded stomach. 'Because it's here to stay. I couldn't bring myself to do anything illegal, you'd better know that.' She got to her feet and made to walk away before she broke down in front of him. Earl grabbed her hand but she shook him off and went to find Fran and Edie. 'I'm going to bed,' she whispered to Fran. 'See you later.'

Fran took one look at her face and summoned Edie to her feet. 'Come on, we're needed back at the hut.'

'He's what?' Fran exploded. 'Bloody married? Get away.'

Bella burst into tears. 'So what do I do now? Any bright suggestions?'

Edie put her arm around Bella's shoulders as she sobbed. She looked across at Fran, who shook her head in despair. 'God alone knows. But you need to talk to Basil as soon as you can.'

'I will. He's taking me over to see Bobby tomorrow, so I'll tell him on the way back. I won't do it until then in case he accidentally says something to Bobby. I really can't tell him yet. Maybe in time I'll feel able to, but he's got enough to contend with without me upsetting him further.'

'You need to write to your mam as well,' Fran suggested. 'At least put her in the picture and ask her to keep it to herself.'

Bella blew out her cheeks. 'That will be a tough one. Do I tell her the father is married, or what?'

Fran grimaced. 'Not sure about that. Maybe in time but not right away, and I'd keep his race and nationality to yourself for now as well. Wait until you absolutely have to tell her.'

'What, like when I'm in labour?' Bella said, shaking her head. 'God, how has this happened to sensible old me? How stupid could I be?'

Bella gazed out of the window, her mind in its usual turmoil, as Basil drove her over to see Bobby in his Wirral convalescent home. Earl had tried to speak to her this morning before he left to fly across the Channel, but she'd told him there was nothing to talk about. The NAAFI wasn't the most private place to hold a conversation or have an argument and she was still trying to come to terms with everything that had happened. No matter what, apart from Fran and Edie she was on her own, for now anyway. But to her surprise she didn't feel too sad, or even upset, by the fact that Earl was married.

Basil pulled up outside a large two-storey property at the top of a winding driveway. The house was set in stunning grounds with neat flower beds and tall trees. The bay windows all looked out across the gardens, affording nice views from each room.

Basil stopped the engine and turned to Bella. 'Right,' he said. 'I'll leave you here for an hour or so and go and see a mate who lives a few miles up the road. Give me a chance to catch up with him and you and Bobby a chance to catch up with each other. I'll come back for the last half-hour and see how he's doing. Is that okay with you?'

She nodded. 'Very okay, thank you. I'll see you later.' She got out of the car and stared up at the beautiful house as Basil drove back down the drive. She rang the bell and stood back. A nurse in a light blue uniform answered the door and invited her inside. 'Thank you. I've come to see Bobby, er, Robert Harrison,' she said.

'Ah, young Robert, yes, just follow me.' Bella couldn't help but see the look of pity pass over the nurse's face as she turned away and led her to a room on the ground floor. 'He's in here and he told me he's expecting a visitor.' She opened the door and stepped back to let Bella inside and then followed her in.

Bobby was sitting looking out of the window and the nurse turned his wheelchair around so that he was facing Bella. His eyes, still as blue as ever, lit up as she walked towards him. His blond hair had grown out of its regulation short back and sides and he'd got that endearing floppy fringe again that Bella had always loved. He held his hands out as she walked towards him. She grasped them and bent to drop a kiss on his cheek.

'Bella, it's so good to see you again. You have no idea.' His voice sounded full of emotion and his eyes were moist with tears.

'Yes I have, Bobby.' Her heart leapt and she almost choked on her words. 'I feel the same. Thank God you survived.'

'For what it's worth,' he said, pointing to the rolled-up pyjama leg that concealed the stump of his left leg. 'I'm a bit of a mess here.'

She smiled and sat down on a chair beside him. 'You'll do,' she said, and he would, because at that moment she knew for certain that she loved him. 'Have you tried to sing?' she asked. 'The smoke and flames didn't damage your vocal cords or anything?'

'They didn't, and yes I have and I can. I've been doing my scales since I got here. Keeping myself in practice. Did Basil really mean it when he said I might be able to sing with you all again when I'm fully recovered? I'll be fitted with a false leg in time as well, which means I at least could stand up onstage. Oh I know it'll be a long job, but it gives me hope that I may have a future.'

Bella nodded. 'He did indeed. He's coming in to see you for the last half-hour of visiting to have a chat with you. Has your mum been here yet to see you?'

'Yes she has. The driver brings her a couple of times a week. She suggested that I might be able to give piano lessons from home. Something else I could look into to earn a living. One of the downstairs rooms at the house is being converted for me and they are getting a ramp put in at the side of the steps to push me up and down when I'm allowed a visit home.'

'That all sounds very promising,' Bella said, loving the enthusiasm in his eyes. He'd get there; time was a great healer of body and mind. 'What about Alicia? What's happening there?'

'Huh, not a lot,' he said with a scowl. 'I haven't heard a single word from her since her one visit to me in London. She's not even been in touch with my mother; after all she's done for her as well. Mother's disgusted at the way she lied about the baby that never was. She covered up for her at first as she found it embarrassing for them both, but eventually Alicia admitted to her that she'd lied. And you know why, don't you? Because she was jealous of you and me. But now she doesn't want to know. The sooner I'm divorced the better, but it can take ages.'

Bella nodded. 'Yes, I believe so. But while that's going on in the background you have to concentrate on getting better. Do everything they tell you, take all the treatment they can offer. I'll write to you as often as I can. Do remember though that picking post up when we're travelling isn't always easy, so please don't worry if you don't get a reply right away. You'll most likely get two at once. We're off down south next month and will probably be in Kent around Christmas and there's talk of us going over to Europe around the same time.'

'Good for you Bella, you deserve it,' he said, putting on a brave face.

She smiled back. 'I don't know – I'm not keen on going towards the war and I hate sailing too. I might take a month or two out with my mam and Molly towards the end of the year instead as I really miss them. Anyway, we'll have to see.'

Bella knew there was no chance of her going anywhere at that time other than to her mam in Wales as her baby would be due. But if she did, she could write to Bobby and him to her a bit easier at least. He didn't need to know the truth as to why she was in Wales. That would have to do for another time.

Chapter Twenty-Five

Conwy, North Wales, December 1942

At the Welsh farmhouse, Bella shifted uncomfortably on the armchair beside the roaring fire and accepted a mug of steaming tea from Audrey, one of the Geordie land girls.

'Why aye, pet, bet you'll be glad when that's out,' Audrey said. 'It's a whopper. Bet it'll be a boy.'

'No doubt,' Bella said, wincing as the baby kicked. 'Whatever it is it's got massive feet. Thank you for the brew, it's much appreciated.'

'Not much else we can do today. Snow's coming down thick and fast, can't even get to the post office to see if my lad's written to me lately. Ah well, I'll get it soon enough.'

'You will,' Bella said, looking out of the window. Outside she could hear excited shrieks from the three little evacuee boys and Molly, who was helping them build a snowman.

The atmosphere here was lovely. Friendly people who had waited on her hand and foot since she'd arrived, cap in hand, after her mam's reply to the letter Bella had written, telling her she was expecting and due in December. Mam had told her that she had spoken to Ruth, the farmer's wife, and Bella was to get herself to Llandudno station as soon as she was able and she would be met there when she phoned to say she'd arrived.

She'd been made very welcome by everyone and it was so good to see her mam and Molly, who were looking very well. Bella was so glad she'd made her mother come out here. Mary loved being with the kiddies, looking after them and playing with them. They filled the hole left by Betty's death. It was so much better for her to be here than lonely and fretting in Wavertree. And she and Ruth were the very best of friends. Mam hadn't pried too much into who Bella's baby's father was. Bella had told her he was an airman she'd met doing the shows, who was also a singer.

'Is he a Yank?' Mam had asked with pursed lips and a slight air of disapproval.

Bella could see no point in lying. 'Yes, Mam, he is.'

'Hmm, well you'll not be the only one taken in with their smooth talk and silk stockings you know. They're not reliable. Anyway, what will be, eh, Bella?'

'Yes, Mam.' Bella tried not to smile. 'And just so you know, I didn't get any silk stockings, but I know a few that did.'

Mam laughed. 'I can't be angry with you, love. Nothing's like it used to be. It's that bloody Hitler's fault. If he hadn't started this war them Yankees wouldn't be over here, causing chaos with our young women. Anyway, how's young Bobby doing?'

Bella told her that according to his latest letter Bobby was doing much better, and was being allowed home for Christmas for a couple of days, and Mam had nodded her approval.

Basil had kept his promise and been to see Bobby several times when he was within driving distance, keeping up his spirits and leaving him sheet music of songs he'd like him to learn for when he was fit and ready. Basil had taken Bella's baby news as well as could be expected and had kept her secret from Bobby, as instructed.

She'd worked until November but never again with Earl's band, although Earl had worked with Fran and Edie occasionally. They'd told Basil they would rather not, but sometimes when a show was already booked there wasn't a choice. Earl did his bit and then kept himself to himself.

Fran's last letter had told Bella that he'd asked after her and Fran had told him to mind his own business, even though he'd looked very concerned. Fran was furious that he'd got involved with Bella when he was already married. But Bella knew deep down that, even if Earl had been single, he wasn't the one for her. Her heart belonged to Bobby and one day, when this war was over and they could all get back to their normal lives, she hoped there would be a way for her and Bobby to be together.

When Bella had been ready to leave, Basil had dropped her off at a station where she could easily catch a train for Llandudno. Fran and Edie would carry on as the Bryant Sisters until Bella knew what she was going to do once her baby arrived. She'd need a few weeks off at least, and she had to make a decision about her future as well as her child's.

At six thirty on Christmas Eve, Bella went into labour. She'd been niggling all day with odd pains but her waters broke as she was helping to clear the tea table. The little evacuee boys stared in fascination as water pooled on the flagstone floor around her feet.

'Bella's peed herself,' little ginger Georgie shouted gleefully and the other two giggled helplessly. 'She needs the potty,' Georgie added.

'Be quiet, cheeky face,' Molly scolded as Mam and Ruth helped Bella up the stairs and settled her on the bed, where Mam had hurriedly placed rubber mattress protectors and towels earlier when Bella had complained of lower back pain.

Mam helped Bella out of her wet underwear and clothes and found her a cotton nightdress to put on. 'Now, that midwife will never get here tonight on her bike,' she said, going to the window and looking out at the still-falling snow.

'We'll manage,' Ruth reassured her. 'I've delivered lambs and piglets and puppies, so I know what I'm doing.'

'And I had all my three at home and the midwife didn't get there until after two of them were born,' Mam said. 'I'm sure we'll be fine,' she reassured Bella, who looked panic-stricken.

'You stay with her and I'll go down and boil some water to sterilise my scissors,' Ruth said, hurrying out of the room. She was soon back upstairs with a bowl of boiling water and several towels. 'Just off the drying rack, so they're nice and clean and warm.'

Bella groaned and grasped her mam's hand. 'It hurts, really hurts,' she groaned.

Mam nodded. 'It does, my love. But you'll forget all about it when you've got your baby in your arms. Now I'll get the things out that we've bought and then they can be airing.' She busied herself laying out tiny clothes and nappies that had been in a box since they'd bought them in the village a couple of weeks ago. It helped to see the little clothes and know that there would soon be a baby to wear them.

A small wooden cradle that Ruth's husband had made for their own children many years ago had been brought back into service, scrubbed clean and painted in fresh white paint. It was waiting in the corner with sheets and blankets cut down from bed sized ones.

'Molly,' Ruth called downstairs. 'Can you get the little rascals ready for bed, love, and bring them up to their room? Give them a biscuit with their milk and they can leave one out for Father Christmas and a carrot for Rudolph.'

Mam shook her head. 'I can't believe where this year has gone. It doesn't seem like five minutes since we were doing that last year.'

Ruth smiled. 'I know. And we're still no nearer to finding out what happened to their mam – or any other family for that matter.'

'They're so well settled here now though, it would be nothing short of cruel to take them away from you. They love you like a mam, Ruth.'

Ruth smiled. 'The twins call me Mam occasionally when they forget for a moment. Ah well, we'll have to see what happens, once this war is over. I think their mam and grandparents copped it and the authorities may not be able to identify them. Thank God she saw fit to have them evacuated. We love them as our own and while they're under my roof they'll always be well looked after.'

'It just shows how you don't have to give birth to a little 'un to be able to love it and take care of it,' Mam said and Ruth agreed.

Between contractions Bella was aware of the conversation going on between her mam and Ruth. What they said was true – this baby didn't need to be brought up by her; but maybe her mam would help her. They'd have to see. A gentle knock on the door broke her thoughts and Molly popped her head around.

'Right, they're settled. Georgie wants to know if we can call it Baby Jesus if it's a boy.' She grinned. 'That's if it arrives on Christmas Day of course.'

'Oh God, it better bloody arrive before tomorrow,' Bella said, grimacing.

'I hope it does,' Molly said. 'Rather you than me, our Bella. Do either of you two want a cuppa? Audrey's in the kitchen making a pot.'

'We'd love one, thank you,' Mam said. 'But we'll wait a bit to see what happens here. It won't be much longer now and then Bella can have one after it's arrived.'

As Molly left the room Bella put her chin down on her chest and grunted. 'Oh God, I think I want to push.'

'Go on then, chuck,' Mam encouraged. 'Here, squeeze my hand if it helps you to concentrate.'

Ruth moved to the end of the bed and lifted the sheets. She moved Bella's legs and examined her. 'I can see its head. Not long now. It's got a lot of very dark hair.'

'Oh, so did all mine,' Mary said. 'Thick and dark brown, just like their dad. Bet this one will be just like its granddad, eh Bella.'

Bella grunted and pushed again. *Not a chance, Mam*, she thought and gave another huge push and her chunky little boy shot into the world. There was silence as Mam and Ruth stared at him and then at Bella. But only for a moment, and then the baby opened his mouth and exercised his lungs. They sprang into action, cutting the cord and rubbing him dry on a fresh towel. He had light-brown skin and stared at them with big chocolate-brown eyes that looked as though they already held a wealth of knowledge, his button nose wrinkling as his face was wiped clean and his generous lips pouting as he objected strongly.

'Typical boy, doesn't like his face being washed,' Ruth said. 'Look at those little rolls on his legs and arms, what a chunky boy he is. Do you know, Mary, I don't think I've ever seen such a beautiful baby.'

Mary nodded, lost for words. She hadn't been expecting this little fellow at all, but the moment she clapped eyes on her new grandson, Mary fell in love. 'He's gorgeous,' she said softly.

'Can I see him please?' Bella asked.

Mary laughed. 'Of course you can, queen. Well done, my love. He's just bloody lovely.'

Bella looked down at the bundle in her arms. He stared back at her with eyes big and wide, browner than hers, Earl's eyes. He was a miniature Earl and he was hers. A feeling of love overwhelmed her and tears ran down her cheeks. At times she'd thought that she might not have any feelings at all for her baby and that her decision to maybe get it adopted was the best idea all round. But that wasn't an option now.

He was family; hers, and she couldn't part with him. But she still needed to work. That was something she'd need to talk to her mam about, but not right now. She felt exhausted and just wanted to sleep. But another wave of pain washed over her and Ruth announced that the afterbirth was ready to be delivered. Mam took hold of the baby while Ruth attended to Bella.

After Ruth had cleared everything away and Bella was settled with a cup of tea and Molly was sitting on the bed holding her new nephew, Mam asked, 'Do we have a name for this little lad yet?'

Bella nodded. She'd love to give him Earl's surname of Franklin but that wasn't possible as Earl would need to give his permission when the baby was registered and that wouldn't be happening. She was still feeling a bit angry with Earl, but she felt she should give their child a family name.

One of Earl's brothers was called Levi and another one was Scotty. The names had stuck with her. She liked them and, looking at her boy, they'd suit him. If, at a later date, Earl was ever in their son's life, his name could be added, but for now Bella would choose. 'He's going to be called Levi Scott Rogers,' she said with pride. 'It has star quality, as Basil would say. He might be a singer one day with a name like that.'

When Fran and Edie rang the farm on Christmas Day to speak to Bella and wish her a merry Christmas, they got the surprise of their lives. Mam helped Bella down the stairs to speak to her friends and made her sit down on a chair.

'You shouldn't even be out of bed,' she chastised. 'But just this once.'

'Happy Christmas,' Fran's voice came over the crackly line. 'How are you?'

'I'm fine, thank you,' Bella replied. 'Well, we both are.'

'Both?'

'Yep, me and my little boy are just fine,' Bella teased.

'Oh my God, you've had the baby. It's a boy? Is everything okay?'

'Just wonderful,' Bella said. 'I'm being well looked after by Mam and Ruth, who delivered him. Well I'll tell you all about it in a letter. Where are you now?'

'Amazing. Congratulations, Bella. Believe it or not we are in Warrington, at Burtonwood. Then we're off down south and will be in Kent for February.'

Bella was silent for a moment. 'Do me a favour then. Tell Earl he has a son and all is well with both me and the baby. That's all he needs to know for now.'

Chapter Twenty-Six

March 1943

Bella wiped the mist off the train window as it chugged through the Kent countryside. She was on her way to meet Fran and Edie, who had promised to be at Deal railway station waiting for her. It had been one heck of a journey from North Wales, with several train changes and cancellations, but she'd managed and was now on the final leg.

Bella was going back to work and although she would miss her son, she knew he had the best surrogate mother he could wish for in her own mam. Mam had told her that going back to work was the best thing all round. Keeping busy and not wasting her talent was important. Little Levi would be looked after so well by Mam and Molly and everyone else at the farm that Bella knew for sure he'd be spoiled rotten by the time she saw him again. But as long as he was loved, and he would be, that was all that mattered.

She couldn't wait to see her friends and Basil again and there was a possibility that Bobby might be joining them at some point soon. Probably when they went back up north in a month or two, as he couldn't travel alone in a wheelchair to meet up with them down here. She was really looking forward to seeing him again, whenever that might be, and she knew from his letters that he was looking forward to seeing her too.

They kept in touch regularly and it was always a pleasure to hear from him. He knew she'd taken a few weeks off to spend time with her family in Wales and he'd never questioned her about it. One day she would tell him why, but the time wasn't right yet. Maybe once the war ended and everyone was living back where they belonged, she'd do it then.

She couldn't keep her son a secret forever, but for now he had to be. She had used Ruth's box camera to take lots of photos of Levi and she'd sent one to Earl with a covering letter, telling him he didn't have to write back, but that she was sure he'd like to see what his child looked like. She felt less cross with him now that she had her beautiful son.

Earl had written back right away and sent a parcel of baby clothes and some money. He told her he'd wept tears of joy when he saw the photo and he would treasure it forever. One day he hoped to see them both, maybe when the war was over. He'd also told her that Ruby, his sister, whom he'd confided in about Bella and the baby, had written to him and told him his wife had been seen out with other men.

He planned to divorce her when he got back to New Orleans, but he was concerned about his little daughter, so would proceed with caution. Bella had been pleased to hear from him – she knew there would never be a future for them, but she didn't feel quite so abandoned, and the fact that he'd told his sister meant a lot to her too. She was also glad for Levi's sake, as she could tell him about his father and his Aunt Ruby when he was old enough to understand.

As the train slowed down and tooted its arrival at the station, Bella got her bag down from the rack and picked up her handbag and the ever-present gas mask box. *Here we go again*, she thought. She felt a little thrill of excitement at the thought of getting back onstage with her friends.

Last year had been the strangest one of her life yet. Becoming well known on the show circuit, singing with George Formby in her hometown, and giving birth to her son. As she stepped down from the platform with her things she was nearly sent flying by Fran and Edie, who flung their arms around her, both crying at once. She looked up and saw Basil standing behind them, a big welcoming smile lighting up his friendly face.

'Welcome back, Bella,' he said, giving them all a group hug. 'It's so good to see you again. I'm a very happy man. My Bryant Sisters are complete once more.'

A Letter from Pam Howes

I want to say a huge thank you for choosing to read *The Girls of Victory Street*. If you did enjoy it, and want to keep up to date with all my latest releases, just sign up at the following link. Your email address will never be shared and you can unsubscribe at any time.

www.bookouture.com/pam-howes

To my loyal band of regular readers who bought and reviewed the Lark Lane stories, thank you for waiting patiently for my new series. I hope you'll enjoy meeting and getting to know my new characters, Bella, Fran and Edie, and their families. Your support is most welcome and very much appreciated. As always, a big thank you to Beverley Ann Hopper and Sandra Blower and the members of their FB group Book Lovers, and Deryl Easton and the members of her FB group The NotRights. Love you all for the support you show me.

A huge thank you to team Bookouture, especially my lovely editorial team, Maisie and Martina, for your support and guidance and always being there – you're the best – and thanks also to the rest of the fabulous staff. Thanks also to my wonderful copy-editor Jacqui and excellent proofreader Loma.

And last, but most definitely not least, thank you to our wonderful media girls, Kim Nash and Noelle Holten, for everything you do for us. And thanks also to the gang in the Bookouture

Authors' Lounge for always being there. As always, I'm so proud to be one of you.

I hope you loved *The Girls of Victory Street* and if you did I would be very grateful if you could write a review. I'd love to hear what you think, and it makes such a difference helping new readers to discover one of my books for the first time. I love hearing from my readers – you can get in touch on my Facebook page, through Twitter, Goodreads or my website.

Thanks,
Pam Howes

 Pam Howes Books

 @PamHowes1

Acknowledgements

As always, my man, my daughters, son-in-law, grandchildren and their wives and partners. Thank you for just being you. It goes without saying that I love you all very much. Thanks to my lovely friends for your support and friendship. A big thank you to Brenda Thomasson and Sue Hulme for Beta reading this story. Thanks to all the members of Stockport Rock'n'Roll Society for being great friends as well as readers. And last but by no means least, a huge thank you to all the wonderful bloggers and reviewers who have supported my Mersey Trilogy and the Lark Lane series. It's truly appreciated. xxx

Printed in Great Britain
by Amazon

55897934R00130